THE
MISADVENTURES
OF THE FAMILY
FLETCHER

THE MISADVENTURES OF THE FAMILY FLETCHER

DANA ALISON LEVY

DELACORTE PRESS

Text copyright © 2014 by Dana Alison Levy
Jacket art copyright © 2014 by Rebecca Ashdown

All rights reserved. Published in the United States by Delacorte Press, an imprint of Random House Children's Books, a division of Random House LLC, a Penguin Random House Company, New York.

Delacorte Press is a registered trademark and the colophon is a trademark of Random House LLC.

Visit us on the Web! randomhouse.com/kids

Educators and librarians, for a variety of teaching tools, visit us at RHTeachersLibrarians.com

Library of Congress Cataloging-in-Publication Data
Levy, Dana.
   The misadventures of the family Fletcher / Dana Levy. — First edition.
      pages cm
   Summary: Relates the adventures of a family with two fathers, four adopted boys, and a variety of pets as they make their way through a school year, kindergarten through sixth grade, and deal with a grumpy new neighbor.
   ISBN 978-0-385-37652-5 (hc) — ISBN 978-0-385-37653-2 (ebook) — ISBN 978-0-385-37654-9 (glb) [1. Family life—Fiction. 2. Brothers—Fiction. 3. Schools—Fiction. 4. Neighbors—Fiction. 5. Adoption—Fiction. 6. Humorous stories.] I. Title.
   PZ7.L58257Mis 2014
   [Fic]—dc23
   2013026320

The text of this book is set in 12.2-point Sabon MT.
Book design by Stephanie Moss

Printed in the United States of America
10 9 8 7 6 5 4 3 2 1
First Edition

To Noah and Isabel, who heard this one first,
and to Patrick, who helped me find a room of my own

Chapter One

IN WHICH WE MEET THE FLETCHERS

FROM THE DESK OF JASON FLETCHER

Boys—
Happy First Day of School! Your lunches are on the counter. PLEASE take the one with your name, and only the one with your name, so as to avoid allergic reactions, midday starvation, or the risk of throwing up due to the perceived grossness of your brothers' lunch choices.

Love, Papa

Eli sat on the wooden porch steps, crammed in with his brothers, while Papa fiddled with the camera. On one side, his youngest brother, Frog, was vibrating with excitement. On the other side, the older two weren't as eager.

"Take. The. Picture," Sam said through gritted teeth.

Clearly his patience with the ritual of first-day-of-school photos was wearing thin by sixth grade.

"Got it!"

The line of four boys separated with the force of bowling pins being knocked every which way. The first day of school meant something different to each of them, but whether they were dreading it or dying to get back, no one wanted to stay on the splintery steps any longer than necessary. This was the first year that all four boys were heading off to real school, if kindergarten counted as real. Eli wasn't sure any place where you glued cotton balls on construction paper was real school, but Frog thought it was, and was excited to finally be in the photo. And according to Fletcher Family Rules, the photo had to be taken. So it was.

Certainly the boys didn't look like brothers, apart from the matching grass-stained knees and monogrammed backpacks—Sam with his tan and his surfer shorts; Jax all elbows and knees and wooly black Afro that he refused to cut; Eli slight and freckly-pale with glasses; and Frog, the size of an average four-year-old, despite being six. Frog seemed to have the energy of at least three six-year-olds, but in a very concentrated size.

Eli fidgeted with his backpack and watched as Jax ran into the yard and punted the bright orange soccer ball that had been sitting in the middle of the lawn. It sailed neatly over the low shrub and into the new neighbor's yard, where it stuck deep in a prickly-looking bush.

"No!" Sam looked up from his phone screen. "That's my favorite ball! And you know he's going to be a total jerk about it. Why'd you do that?" He moved to slug Jax, but Jax dodged quickly out of the way. Eli figured Jax's speed always increased around 20 percent when he was avoiding being whacked by Sam.

"Sorry! I'll go grab it," Jax said.

"No! Nobody go anywhere. Sam, we have approximately three million other soccer balls around here, and we need to launch. But, Jax, we have given repeated warnings." Papa's voice came from behind the porch chair, where he had dropped his camera lens cap. "I know you miss having the Kellehers next door. We were all sorry when they moved. But for better or worse, we have Mr. Nelson now. And he does *not* appreciate the balls, street-hockey pucks, and other items that you keep sending over. After the rather difficult conversation with Officer Hollis on Labor Day, the less we bug Mr. Nelson, the better."

Eli knew he wasn't kidding. When the family had come home from their vacation last month, the Kelleher house had no longer had the FOR SALE sign swinging in front of it. Instead of a basketball hoop, the driveway now had nothing but an extremely shiny old Buick. And the yard, which had been remarkable only for the dandelions, was now all spruced up with what looked like hundreds of carefully transplanted flowers. Flowers that apparently weren't able to withstand the occasional ball. Old Mr. Nelson didn't seem as fancy as his flowers—he was kind of grizzled-looking. He scowled at the boys when he walked his yappy little dog and ignored them the rest of the time. But calling the police on their sing-along had definitely been what Eli's history book would call an escalation.

"Why couldn't someone cool with kids have moved in?" Jax mumbled.

No one bothered to answer him.

"Papa! Is it time to go? Will my name tag say 'Frog'?" Frog jumped up and down in excitement. "Or will it say 'Jeremiah'? I hate it when it says my real name."

"Don't worry, Froggie," said Jax helpfully. "They'll probably just call you Doofus."

"They will not!" Frog retorted. "And, Papa, do you think they'll keep the seat next to mine saved for Flare? He's coming today too, you know."

Papa ignored the mention of Flare, Frog's imaginary best friend, who happened to be a cheetah, and concentrated on shutting down his camera. Eli agreed with this strategy. It was never a good idea to try to talk Frog out of his imaginary creatures.

Once the camera was carefully placed back in its case, the launch began in earnest. This year Sam and Jax would bike or walk together most of the time, but today, with all the school supplies, they rode with Papa. Eli had a little pang that he and Jax weren't starting fourth grade together. They had always been in the same grade at the

4

same school, even if they hadn't been in the same class, and he would miss the comfort of having Jax nearby. But changing schools had been his choice; he wasn't going to worry about it now. Sam and Jax milled around, double-checking binders and colored pencils, while Papa tried to figure out where he had left his keys. Frog, who was supposed to get into the car with Eli, was—ugh—licking his hand and smoothing down his dark wispy hair in an effort to make it stay flat. Finally he climbed in and started to buckle his booster seat.

Eli watched all this from his own seat, buckled in and waiting patiently for Dad to get in and take him to Narnia, to Hogwarts, to Never Land. Eli was starting a new school this fall, one for gifted students, and he was more than ready.

He opened the car door and shouted out, "Dad? You're driving me, right? I don't want to be late!"

"Close the door! Flare is getting chilly!" Frog commanded. Eli ignored him.

"I'm coming, Eli," Tom Anderson, known to the boys as Dad, answered as he walked down the driveway. He got into the van, clutching his coffee mug with one hand while trying desperately to shove his lunch into his briefcase with the other. "We just have to drop Frog off first. You'll be there in plenty of time. I'm just hoping *I* will— I have a department meeting before my first class. But your school's on the way to Middleton High. Sort of.

Well, it's not the opposite direction." He sighed, giving up and dropping the lunch onto the already cluttered passenger seat of the van. His coffee spilled slightly as it fell with a clunk on an acorn that was destabilizing the cup holder.

"Craaa . . . napple," he muttered, trying to keep the coffee off his papers.

"Dad! Was that a rude word?" Eli asked, straining forward against his seat belt. "No rude words in front of us! You owe a quarter to the Rude Box."

"No. It was 'cranapple.' There's nothing rude about 'cranapple.' It's a kind of juice." Dad reversed the car out of the driveway. "Okay. Off to Froggie's kindergarten. I can't wait to see your classroom!"

Eli sighed. It had been four months and twenty-eight days, or approximately 216,000 minutes, since he'd found out he'd been admitted to Pinnacle. He guessed a little longer wouldn't matter.

Chapter Two

IN WHICH JAX CONSIDERS SURVIVAL OF THE FITTEST

FROM THE DESK OF JASON FLETCHER

Jax—

Congratulations! By forgetting to scoop the litter box, you've inspired Zeus to branch out. He has returned to his wildcat roots and peed in Dad's potted ficus plant in the living room. Over to you to clean it up and explain to Dad.

Love, Papa

Jax was freaking out, just a little. It was the first day of fourth grade, and everything depended on Sam. Sam was royalty, kind of like a carnivore with a bunch of gazelles and zebras and wildebeests around him. As a sixth grader, he was already the top of the food chain, but Sam was also the best goalie the Shipton soccer coach had seen in ages; the talk was that Sam might even make the Elite Team next year. And he was funny. Funny like he made Jax snort milk out of his nose at least once a week at dinner, which actually hurt more than Jax would have thought. Everyone loved Sam.

No one loved Jax.

Well, to be fair, no one knew him. Jax had spent third grade hidden in the world of Star Wars, drawing battle scenes with his best friend, Henry, during every recess and debating who would win various superhero fights. Sometimes Eli had joined them, and he'd always had cool ideas for battles, though usually he'd been too busy reading some crazy book to bother with them. Although he didn't really think about it a lot, Jax knew having a total genius brother like Eli in the same grade didn't exactly help his coolness factor. Guiltily, he was kind of relieved Eli had wanted to switch schools this year. Of course, he would always stand up for Eli if other kids teased him. Still, it would be easier to be cool with Sam as the only other Fletcher in the building.

This year could be different. Sure, Star Wars was still awesome, but he'd now read all the Harry Potter books and seen most of the movies, and had even seen a PG-13 movie with a babysitter who hadn't known he wasn't allowed. And, most importantly, unlike the third graders, the fourth graders were in the Upper Elementary, which meant Jax would be in the same building as Sam. He could be cool this year. *If* Sam backed him up. If he treated Jax as a goober the first week of school, all was lost.

It was time to take action. Still thinking about carnivores, Jax pictured the remoras that swam alongside the huge sharks, helping them out by eating any bugs and dirt and stuff that stuck to them. Not that he wanted to eat bugs off Sam. But maybe he could make himself useful.

"Hey, Sam?" Jax asked, peering over the back of the front passenger seat, where Sam was finally allowed to sit. "I know it's your night to walk Sir Puggleton, but if you want, I'll do it. When we get home, I mean. Just remind me."

"Thanks, J. That'd be great," Sam answered absently, not looking up from his phone, where he was still texting. He'd gotten it for his birthday that summer, and it seemed to be attached to his hand.

"And, um . . . if you want, I'll do it next time too. I don't mind." Jax thought about offering to take over Sam's litter box duties as well, since the boys traded off, but he really hated litter box duty. He'd save that in case he needed it.

There was no answer from the front seat, though Jax saw Papa's eyes swivel toward him in the rearview mirror.

Jax avoided Papa's glance. Papa would *not* get the need to be on Sam's good side, and would launch into a lecture that would include references to some philosophers,

Walt Whitman (his favorite poet), and the Beatles. But Papa worked from home, creating some kind of wizard-like technical computer models, so what did he know? He hadn't even met most of the people he worked with—they were off in China or India or across the country in California. Dad taught high school history. He would understand the survival of the fittest.

Jax was desperate. If only he could make his brother crack up, or impress him in some way before they got to school . . . Something! The car stopped at a red light, and as they sat, Jax looked at the leafy green trees that lined the streets of their historic town.

"Hey! What's black and white and red all over?" he asked, hoping his voice didn't sound as panicked as he felt.

"A newspaper," said Papa automatically.

"A zebra," answered Sam at the same time.

"Nope! A skunk in a blender!" Jax started laughing hysterically. Oh, no. It was happening. The nervous hysterical laughter that led to tears, then the hiccups. This was the worst.

The car lurched forward, and Sam turned around.

"Jax? You okay, man? Breathe, dude, breathe! You sound like you're dying." Sam had finally put down his phone. "What's up? Are you nervous about Upper El? It's not that different, seriously. Just remember, most kids are going to play football at recess. If you want to be totally down, start bringing your own ball. Some dorks play four square, but trust me, you don't want to do that."

Papa snorted. "Please, Samuel," he said. "Tell me you didn't just judge a kid's coolness on whether he throws a football or a rubber ball during your fifteen minutes on the playground."

Sam shrugged. "I don't make the rules, but it's true. Jax'll see it for himself. I'm just trying to help."

Jax shook his head, willing himself to get a grip. Slowly he breathed in through his nose, out through his mouth, the way Jedis did when preparing for battle. No hiccups. Thank goodness.

"I'm not nervous," he said faintly, wondering how he could possibly explain. He just wanted Sam to . . . to . . .

Too late. They pulled up in a line of cars at the school.

"Have a marvelous Monday, boys," Papa said as they unpacked themselves from the car. "Jackson, enjoy Upper El—I can't wait to hear about it." Then he drove away.

Jax gave a faint wave, not wanting to look too eager, and stood on the sidewalk. He peered around the playground, wondering where Henry was. When he stepped forward, he tripped and flew against the curb, his backpack jouncing up and hitting him in the head before he landed, hard, on his hands and knees on the asphalt. He quickly rolled and performed an impressive almost-somersault, and landed back on his feet before five seconds had passed. Panting, he stood up, looking around frantically to see if anyone had noticed. What a disaster! He couldn't imagine a worse start, unless he had barfed on his shoes like Teddy had done back in first grade. Trying to be inconspicuous, Jax picked bits of bloody gravel out of the palm of his hand. Luckily, it didn't look like anyone had seen him. Carefully he walked forward into the playground.

Sam had already found his crowd and was engaging in a complicated series of fist bumps with his best friend, Tyler, and five other guys. They all looked enormous, way taller than Jax, who was still hoping for a growth spurt. Before Jax could move, his brother walked over and slung an arm over his shoulder.

"Guys, little Jax is at Upper El this year. If you see him around, give him a noogie for me!"

Sam noogied Jax's kinky black hair, and the rest of the boys followed suit, as though rubbing Jax's head were some new rite of passage. By the time they were done, Jax knew he probably looked like he'd been struck by lightning, but he didn't care. He could see the rest of the fourth graders clustered in a corner of the school garden, staring enviously at him as he joked and high-fived Sam's friends. It had happened—he was cool.

Chapter Three

IN WHICH ELI IS READY FOR THE PINNACLE WAY

FROM THE DESK OF TOM ANDERSON

Eli—

Enjoy your lunch. Look up. Smile. Talk to someone sitting nearby. Your book will still be there when you look down again.

Love, Dad

According to Eli's calculations, Dad had been in Frog's classroom for sixteen minutes, which was 960 seconds. But due to some phenomenon—he thought it was called cognitive dissonance, but he wasn't sure—it felt like at least an hour. He thought about tapping the horn, just lightly, the way Dad did when Papa went into the gourmet store for French bread and then wound up staying in there talking about cheese with the owners for twenty minutes. But Eli didn't dare. Touching the horn was NOT ALLOWED in the Fletcher household, ever since Jax and Henry had held a contest to see who could hit it harder and had managed to get it stuck. It had happened the day after they'd gotten back from vacation, and Mr. Nelson had roared, threatening to call the police. Eli had thought it was ridiculous. It wasn't like *they'd* enjoyed the forty-five minutes it had taken to find the right fuse to turn the thing off any more than he had.

Seventeen minutes (1,020 seconds). Enough! Eli had been waiting all summer long for school to start. The Pinnacle School . . . even the name was exciting. Unlike his old school, Grove Lower Elementary, Pinnacle sounded like something worth working toward. Not that the Grove school was all bad. Sitting out here, watching the little kids stream in, Eli kind of missed his friends. But they weren't here now. Miles and Teddy and Jamil had moved on with Jax to Upper Elementary, and while that could have been cool, he knew the Pinnacle School was where he really belonged. The words he'd memorized from the school brochure rolled around in his head: *For exceptional academically focused students who are seeking a superlative intellectual experience. There are many different paths to a happy life. The Pinnacle School is exclusively for those who believe their path is found through academic rigor.*

Eli's brothers had laughed, of course. In fact, Sam had made a dinner table game of rewriting the brochure. "For exceptional geeks focused on finding other goobers who want to watch paint dry" had been just one of his contributions.

Eli had ignored him. A school where everyone was the smart kid sounded awesome. A school where he didn't get "rewarded" for already knowing the work by being allowed to sit and read quietly in the corner. Not that he didn't like having reading time—he did. In fact, he had read the entire Percy Jackson series sitting in that corner, despite the fact that those books weren't on the approved third-grade reading list.

The car door opened and Dad climbed in, pulling his tie back into place. Doubtless, Frog's goodbye hugs had been the cause of the disheveling.

"Okeydokey, Eli. You ready?" he asked. "Frog is officially launched in kindergarten. His teacher even made a cozy stall for Flare to enjoy while Frog is working, so she's clearly up to the job. Now let's get you to the pinnacle!" He laughed a little at his own joke and reached back to pat Eli's knee.

"Are you nervous? New school and all that? You know it'll—"

Eli cut him off. "I'm not nervous at all," he said. And it was true. He looked down at his T-shirt, with a scientific diagram of a stingray and a fake name tag that said HI, MY

NAME IS RAY on it. At his old school no one had found the shirt funny, no matter how many times he had tried to explain it. He was sure plenty of kids would laugh about it at Pinnacle. Still, starting anything new was a little stressful. He suspected his heart rate was slightly elevated, and wondered if he should mention it to Dad. No, he decided, better not. After all, he had begged for a chance to change schools, had asked what he could do to help pay for it, had promised to get a paper route or walk dogs or something to raise money. His parents hadn't been sure it was the right choice, but he knew it was. And finally they had agreed. No reason to make them doubt that now.

They were heading out of their small ocean city of Shipton and toward the highway. The Pinnacle School was two exits down the interstate, a trip that Eli had to admit wasn't as fun as walking or biking with Sam and Jax, which he would have been allowed to do this year if he had gone to Upper Elementary. It was nearly twenty minutes before they got to their exit and wound through the industrial park where the school was located.

The school had been founded only ten years earlier, and the founders had clearly believed that the best learning happened with limited distractions. There was barely any outdoor play space, although the school was near a kind of marshy wetland that Eli thought must be good for birds and turtles and such. The little space there was had clearly defined areas with signs that said EXERCISE SPACE

16

and QUIET RECREATION SPACE. For a moment Eli thought back to the Grove school's messy playground with four square, a rope spiderweb, monkey bars, and swings. No question it had been a distraction.

Eli and Dad got out of the car together, Dad trying to smooth his curly hair and tuck in the back of his shirt, which had gotten wrinkled in the car. Eli couldn't help wishing Dad weren't quite so messy. On the other hand, if Papa had dropped him off . . . Eli shuddered at the thought. Since Papa worked from home, he had been known, on rainy days, to drive to school still wearing his pajamas. Certainly Dad was the safer choice for a new school.

As they walked toward the entrance, carefully staying on the brick path, Eli looked up and saw the school motto carved into the stone above the door in scrolling Latin. *"Aut disce aut discede,"* Dad read. Then he laughed. "Do you know what that means?" he asked Eli. When Eli shook his head, Dad said, "It means, 'Either learn or leave.' Interesting motto."

Eli just smiled. He had no doubts. This was the right place for him.

Chapter Four

IN WHICH THE SCHOOL DAY IS DISCUSSED

Tyler cell:
Dude im stoked for socket meet in yard at 4 k.
Socket. Sprocket. SOCCER. Stupid phone.

The biggest problem with September, in Sam's estimation, was that it still felt like August. It had to be eighty degrees out, he figured as he and Jax walked home from school. Jax was all fired up about his locker with a door, the ice cream vending machine in the cafeteria, and the promise of launching bottle rockets in science later in the year. Fourth grade had exceeded his expectations so far.

Sam didn't share his brother's excitement. Sixth grade, he'd decided, was one big lecture about how grades were really starting to matter. In fact, his English teacher, who was particularly rabid on the subject, had walked the class through a what-if exercise that had taught them that they ignored his assignments at their peril, since it could lead to a failing mark, a repeat of sixth grade, and the inability to ever go to college. This outcome seemed a bit harsh for not reading *Johnny Tremain*, but Sam hadn't been about to argue with someone whose tie had come loose and whose shirt had come untucked from the effort of threatening them.

At least September also meant the start of soccer, which was more than a consolation prize for school. Still, even soccer was making him nervous now, and soccer *never* made him nervous. This coming spring the players would be chosen for the Shipton Under-15 Elite Team. If Sam made it, he'd be the youngest player on the team in at least five years. And he had a chance. He just had to stay focused.

"Jax, want to take shots on me when we get home? After you walk Sir Puggleton, I mean?" Sam had to admit, Jax had a pretty tough shot, when it was actually near the net. Unfortunately, they often went wide. One of his shots had careened across the bushes and hit the new neighbor's ancient dog as it had been getting out of the car.

"And you need to get my ball back from Mr. Nelson. Good luck with that. He's a serious waste of space, that guy. Did you hear him yesterday? He yelled at Dad for mowing the lawn. At NOON! Who freaks out if it's noisy at noon?" Sam shook his head, disgusted with stupid neighbors, crazy teachers, and the rest of his life.

"Sure," Jax said. "But what about homework? I heard Tyler talking about some kind of book report."

Sam made a kind of hissing noise in the back of his throat. Fletcher Family Rules said that everyone's homework was done first, and nobody could play until all the work was done, even if everyone else was waiting for you.

It was an effective strategy. There was nothing like a bunch of brothers breathing down your neck to get the ideas flowing. Sam himself had threatened to hawk phlegm into Eli's drink if he didn't wrap up his research and *finish* already. Sixth grade was off to an unpleasant start.

Three hours later, sweaty and mud-covered, Sam was feeling much better about things. Tyler had wandered over, Eli and Dad had arrived home just a few minutes after Sam had finished his report, and after an hour of Tyler and Jax taking shots on him, with Eli gamely defending, Sam was pretty confident about the first team practice tomorrow. He waved goodbye to Tyler just as Dad came outside.

"Guys! Time to eat!" Dad said, standing on the back deck waving a pair of tongs at them to get their attention.

Mr. Nelson, who was cutting roses from his bushes into a careful bouquet, scowled over at them. Sam couldn't help noticing how carefully his neighbor examined each rose before cutting it and adding it to the bunch. The dude was weird, that was for sure.

"First-day-of-school dinner! Yes!" Eli and Jax raced each other to the house, jostling and shoving the whole way. Fletcher Family Rules held that everybody got his favorite food on the first and last days of school.

Once inside, Sam kicked off his muddy cleats and elbowed his brother out of the bathroom.

"Move it, Stink. You've been in here for five minutes already!" He shut the door behind Jax, who was still arguing over whether the last goal should be disqualified because of a foul.

The sink was brown with the accumulated dirt of three pairs of hands, and Sam wiped it down the drain with absentminded conscientiousness. By the time he'd finished washing his face and peering into the mirror to see if any hairs were beginning to sprout on his upper lip, the rest of the family was seated.

"Finally!" Eli said, staring at his plate with the intensity of a hunting dog pointing a kill. "I think I'm suffering from addiction withdrawal symptoms! I haven't had dumplings in at least two weeks."

Eli's first- and last-day meals were always the same: Chinese dumplings and spareribs that Dad—and now Eli too—picked up on the way home from school. Sam's was spaghetti and meatballs, with real, homemade, cook-all-day-and-make-the-house-smell-awesome sauce. Of course, at the moment, the house didn't smell like anything but sweaty boys since Papa had just defrosted the sauce he'd frozen on the last day of school. Still, it was delicious. Frog was happy with instant macaroni and cheese. ("In the purple box, not the blue box. . . . The blue box is disgusting!" he would tell anyone who was around.) And Jax changed his mind each time. Tonight it was lobster and mashed potatoes.

For a moment the table was silent except for the snuffling, chewing, and swallowing of all the different meals. Even Dad got his food choice, since it was his first day of school too: rare grilled steak with mushrooms and peppers. Papa had a small portion of everyone's meal, making, he said, a most fascinating study in how something can be less than the sum of its parts. Finally the eating slowed, and Papa spoke.

"So, who's going first? Eli, do you want to tell us about your new school?"

The only answer was a snuffling grunt as Eli, who weighed less than Sam's soccer bag, shoved his seventh dumpling into his mouth.

Papa grimaced slightly and turned away. "Okay. We'll get back to you when you've finished inhaling your food. What about you, Frog-o? You already gave me the rundown when I picked you up, but tell Dad and your brothers about kindergarten."

Frog grinned, his mouth ringed in a cheesy rim. "So good! And Flare loved it too. He has a special seat. And I made a new friend. Her name is Ladybug Li and she has three sisters and two moms!"

The rest of the table paused and looked at Frog, who continued eating, happily oblivious. Frog had what his preschool teacher had called an engaging and encompassing imaginary world, which Sam figured pretty much meant he was nuts. Papa and Dad, of course, thought an imaginary cheetah under the bed was perfectly normal. And they didn't think it was odd when for six months last year Frog had told everyone he had a younger brother named Connecticut who was only two but could read. The worst part was that several people had believed him, which to Sam just showed how weird his family was.

Dad spoke first. "That's nice. Did you meet any other kids?"

Sam could tell Dad was avoiding asking if Frog had met any "real" friends. Frog could get very touchy if you tried to call him on his imaginary world.

"Yup." Frog nodded. "I was in a group with Grace and Isabelle and Rob and Noah and another Noah. Isabelle tried to bite another girl, but mostly she's nice. They were all mostly pretty nice, except for the second Noah. He cried. Then he barfed. Then his mom came."

There was another moment of silence as they all considered the unfortunate Noah.

"Did you learn anything? Did your teachers start teaching you to read?" This came from Eli, who was quite concerned that his youngest brother was only sounding out words, despite their fathers' assurances that this was completely age appropriate.

"Yeah, we did the alphabet, and thought about words that start with *A*. I said 'airplane.'"

"'Aerodynamic,'" said Eli automatically.

"'Alligator,'" chimed in Papa.

"'Ass—'" Sam began.

"Samuel!" Papa and Dad said together.

"What?" Sam couldn't keep a grin from spreading across his face, though he tried to look innocent. "I was going to say 'assassinate.' What did you think I was going to say?"

Jax burst out laughing, spitting lobster across the table, and a chorus of groans arose. Sam couldn't help snickering.

Papa fixed him with the stink-eye and said, "Since you're so full of linguistic enrichment, why don't you tell us a bit about sixth grade?"

Sam's snort of laughter died down. It's-time-to-get-serious sixth grade wasn't really something he felt like talking about. He shrugged. "It was fine. The usual. Tyler and Connor and Josh are in my homeroom. I have Mr. Washbar for language arts, and he was apoplectic—another good *A* word, Frog—about how our grades start to really matter this year. According to him, if we don't work hard on our English papers, we're probably going to wind up living in cardboard boxes."

"Well," said Dad. "That's a bit extreme. But he does have a point. Depending on how you do this year, your middle school classes will be different, which will then affect your high school classes, and so on."

Papa gave a quiet snort that everyone heard anyway. No one needed to ask him why. Papa had dropped out of college his freshman year to start building a computer model full-time. He'd eventually sold it to some huge company for pots of money, which he'd promptly invested in some African water company. Then he'd invented something else and sold *it*. He was less impressed with grades and classes than Dad was.

"Whatever," Sam said. He inhaled another bite of dinner and swallowed it faster than seemed possible. "I'll work hard. Obviously. But I'm still more worried about the Shipton Elite Team tryouts in the spring. They went to the Massachusetts state finals last year—they're really good. I mean, school's important and all, but this is soccer!" He smiled as if he were joking, but he didn't really feel like it was a joke. Making that team as an almost–seventh grader would be the most epic thing ever.

Mercifully, Papa and Dad turned their attention to Jax.

"And what about fourth grade?" Dad asked. "Anything special going on there? We got an email about a yearlong research project your grade is doing."

Jax nodded, swallowing his bite of lobster. "It's called the Veteran Project. It's pretty cool. We find a veteran and interview them, and research them using Google and stuff, and write about what war they fought in. We're getting this whole timeline of when everything's due. We start it soon, but most of the work isn't until after winter vacation and the final report is due in the spring. But anyway, the best reports will even be printed in the paper! It would be sick if I won."

He was quiet for a minute. "Do we know any veterans?"

"That's a tough one," Dad said. "I actually had a few uncles who served, but one of them died in combat when I was too young to really know him, and the other has never been willing to talk about it."

Sam said, "I think Tyler's got a cousin or something who's over in the Middle East. But I guess she's not a veteran yet. She's still fighting."

"Well, we can think about it," Papa said. "But it sounds like an interesting project. Whether or not you agree with all the wars we've been in, the fact is that these soldiers have interesting stories."

"Mr. Nelson's a veteran," Eli said, raising his face from his plate for the first time. "He has those special license plates and a sticker on his car that says VIETNAM VETERANS: NEVER FORGET."

Sam and Jax groaned at the same time. And before either parent could say anything more, Jax started telling everyone about his locker and all the other treasures of fourth grade, and the dinner proceeded peacefully.

It wasn't until Sam and Frog were taking their turn loading the dishwasher that Sam realized they had never heard about Eli's new school.

Chapter Five

IN WHICH THE FLETCHERS STORM THE PINNACLE SCHOOL

Eli—

    I'm really, really sorry. I know you're mad, but I am sorry. I can try to help fix it (if you tell me how). Really. Please don't stay mad. Please?

                      Your loving brother,

                      Jax

P.S. I know it was my idea, but it was Frog who did it. You don't seem mad at him.

September passed in a blur of soccer practices, back-to-school barbecues, and increasingly difficult homework, and Eli was amazed to realize he'd been at the Pinnacle School for nearly a month already. It was Family Night, an opportunity for Pinnacle students to showcase their academic efforts to date. At least, that was what the flyer said. Eli wasn't sure exactly what he was supposed to showcase. There had been plenty of work, that was true. But it wasn't like he had stuff to show off—no Popsicle-stick buildings or alphabet cutouts like Frog's class, or even drawings of different penguins to scale like Jax's class. (Interestingly, the emperor penguin was almost exactly the same height as Jax himself.)

Still, it was exciting to have his whole family there at the school. Sam was still wearing his soccer clothes, having come straight from practice, but the rest of them were dressed normally, to Eli's relief. Even Papa had managed to put on a pair of jeans and a T-shirt that didn't say anything embarrassing.

"This is where we do outdoor recreation, and over there is where we observe wildlife," Eli told his brothers, pointing to the clearly marked areas. "There are some really cool—"

Frog cut him off. "Where's the playground?" he asked.

"Um . . . there really isn't one. That area there"—he pointed toward a fenced-in area—"is where we can play tag or something."

Frog looked incredulous, and Jax stopped bugging Sam.

"No playground?" Frog asked. He sounded like he didn't quite believe it.

"But you play sports!" Jax said. "How can you stand it?"

Thankfully, Dad broke in. "Pinnacle School is for

students who choose to focus more exclusively on the academic side of the school experience, and Eli gets plenty of time for sports and running around after school. It suits Eli; it doesn't matter if you knuckleheads like it or not. Now please be gracious guests and let E-man show us around. Eli, take it away."

They trooped into the school, silently taking in the solemn hallways, empty of the kids' artwork and motivational posters that lined the halls of the other boys' schools. The only art on the walls were gold-framed portraits of famous scholars.

Eli heard Papa whisper to Dad, "Instant history—are we supposed to think that these people went here?"

Dad answered mildly, "Since we just passed Albert Einstein, I think we can assume they're just here as inspiration. This is Eli's new school, a place he chose. Let's just . . . admire it."

Up ahead his brothers were having sliding contests down the empty hall, Sam's cleats clacking on the floor. Most of the students and their families were already in the classrooms. Eli led everyone to his doorway, which bore a small plaque that read MS. GALLWIN: FOURTH GRADE.

After opening the door, the Family Fletcher slid in as quietly as they could, which wasn't particularly quietly at all.

Eli had been so worried about what his family would

think of his school that he hadn't really thought about how the school would react to his family. But as they trooped in, Eli couldn't help seeing them through new eyes. Dad, extremely tall, perpetually rumpled, with his light brown hair in his eyes and his glasses constantly smudged; Papa, as tall as Dad but probably twice as wide, with his jeans and T-shirt, his head shaved as bald as an egg; and of course all his brothers. Tall and short, pale and brown, they all clattered in. Ms. Gallwin stopped talking and stared.

Eli nervously scratched inside his ear, until Sam smacked his hand down.

"Um . . . sorry we're late, Ms. Gallwin. My brother had soccer. These are my dads"—he gestured behind him—"and my brothers." Hoping desperately that was enough of an introduction, Eli swooped into his seat.

Ms. Gallwin swallowed and recovered herself. "Ah, Mr. Fletcher and . . ." She hesitated. In the seats, dozens of grown-ups stared blankly at the Fletchers, who were squeaking chairs and shoving desks out in an attempt to seat themselves.

Papa stepped forward, smiling. "I'm Jason Fletcher— please call me Jason. And this is my husband, Tom Anderson."

Dad reached out his hand, also smiling. They had been through this many times, Eli knew. Still, Eli had been Frog's age the last time any of them had started a new school. Since then they'd all been going, one after another, through Grove Lower Elementary and Grove Upper Elementary. By now the Fletchers were a known, and mostly loved, element. Other than the principal and the third-grade teacher who had shown them around last spring, no one knew them here.

Eli stared at his spotless desk, his face burning. He wasn't embarrassed about his family—it wasn't that. It was just . . . there were so many of them. And so many boys. He knew the questions were coming.

Sure enough, as soon as Ms. Gallwin had wrapped up her welcome speech, which had sounded rather wan and confused by the time the Fletchers had all seated themselves, Eli's classmates gathered around him.

"Are those guys all your brothers? How old are they?" Griffin said.

"Well, Sam is twelve. Jax is the same age as me, almost—" Eli started, but Jax interrupted.

"I'm actually older. I was ten in April, and Eli wasn't ten until August," he said.

"And Frog just turned six," Eli finished. He hoped this was the end of it.

"You guys don't look anything alike," Griffin said. It was hot in the room, and Eli could see sweat beading under Griffin's reddish curls.

"Duh." Ambrose, a tall boy with a Korean National

Soccer shirt answered before Eli could say anything. "Have you ever heard of adoption?"

Eli was grateful that Ambrose had jumped in.

"Um, yeah, Griffin. We're all adopted," Eli said, edging toward Dad, who was reading the compositions taped to the wall. Eli hoped that the questions would stop now. But before he walked away, he heard Mika say, in a loud whisper, "Why do they have *two* dads? Don't they have a mom?"

It was apparently loud enough for Frog to hear too, and before Eli could answer, Frog spoke up. "Of course we had moms! Don't you even know how babies are made? It takes a man and a woman, and the egg meets the—"

"Okay! Frog! Yes, everyone does have a mom and dad. Thanks," Sam said. Luckily, he was standing close enough to cut Frog off before he gave the whole fourth-grade class a full lesson in reproductive biology.

Eli exhaled in a gasp as Sam continued, answering Mika, Griffin, and the others who had crowded around.

"We were all adopted as babies. Our dads have been together for ages. They got married two years ago—"

"We all went skiing in Colorado for the honeymoon!" Frog interrupted.

"And most of us go to school in Shipton," Sam finished. His voice, as his younger brothers knew, had shifted to slightly menacing. "Do you have any other questions? Want to know our birthdays? Or height and weight?"

Griffin, who obviously didn't have older brothers, ignored the menace. "Yeah. Why did two guys—"

Ambrose cut him off. "Come *on,* Griffin. Let's show your parents our model solar panel for the solar-powered bike." He looked slightly embarrassed as he dragged Griffin back toward their parents, who were chatting in a group near the whiteboard. Relieved that the worst was over, Eli joined Dad and Papa by the essays.

"This is really fascinating, bud. Did you get to choose the topic yourself?" Dad asked.

Eli nodded, a glow of pride starting to replace the nervous feeling. "We're allowed to choose anything at all for our weekly research essays, as long as it's academic in nature. And if we're really interested, we can continue the same topic for up to three weeks. Then we have to find something new. So I spent two weeks on that one: 'Why Bridges Stay Up.' It was fascinating."

Dad and Papa exchanged smiles, and Eli smiled too. Maybe the night was going to go well after all.

But just as he thought that, a horrible crash filled the room, followed by immediate silence. Silence that was broken only by the tiny voice of . . . Frog.

"Sorry," the voice said. "I'm really, really sorry!"

Eli turned around.

On the floor was Griffin and Ambrose's solar panel.

A month of work lay in pieces next to Frog, also on the floor, who had obviously decided to try the sliding game again, this time in the classroom.

Eli closed his eyes. Hopefully Family Night was only once a year. Because 365 days wouldn't be long enough before they had to do this again.

Chapter Six

IN WHICH GIRLS AND SOCCER COLLIDE

> **Papa cell:**
> Zeus has fallen out the window again. Mr. Nelson
> was NOT pleased to see me crawling under his
> car in my pajamas—since the cat was long gone,
> I guess I looked pretty suspicious. Anyway, he's
> locked in the bedroom until we can decide a fair
> punishment. (The cat, not Mr. Nelson.)

It was raining, but for Jax, that just made practice better. Soccer in the rain meant absolute freedom to get totally covered in mud, and no one could get mad. Plus, you didn't get so hot. On rainy days he wished he played keeper like Sam; keepers definitely got dirtier than the rest of the team put together.

Jax's team, the Shipton Sailors Under Elevens, was undefeated, which, Eli pointed out, only meant that they had won their first three games. It was pretty good to have

Eli on the same team. Eli wasn't much of a player—he didn't really like to run—but he was sick at figuring out the other team's weakness.

"Watch out for number four," he might say. "He's six inches taller than all of us. If he gets the ball, no one's going to catch him." Or, "Number sixteen looks impressive, but he can't fake. If he tries to fake you, stay on it. Chances are good he'll lose the ball."

Coach Sean said that Eli was more useful than the rest of the team put together, and Coach Nan said that if the other boys paid attention on the sidelines like Eli did instead of rolling around like monkeys on espresso, they might figure some of this stuff out too. Jax was proud of his brother the brain.

It was just that Eli still wasn't talking to him after the solar panel episode. Frog, the little ferret, had told Eli that the sliding contest had been Jax's idea. And now Eli was giving Jax the silent treatment.

Eli's silent treatment could last a loooong time.

"Come on. I said I was sorry. And it's not like *I* broke anything! It was Frog's stupid fault that he went too far!" Jax was hoping for an early thaw, but it wasn't looking good.

Eli went over and sat with Henry, and promptly started whispering. Great. They were about to scrimmage the Under Twelve girls team, and apparently Eli was going to share his wisdom with everyone but Jax.

Jax looked wistfully toward the far field, where Sam was in goal, his team peppering him with shots. Sam could usually joke Eli out of his moods, but today Sam was too busy. Jax was on his own.

The girls' team was taking the field, and Jax stared— they were *huge*. The girls' teams split on even birth years, while the boys took odd years, which meant that half the girls' team was a year older. Jax looked over at Henry in dismay. "Look at Annie. She's like a foot taller than me. I swear we were the same height last year. And check out Olivia. . . . She looks like she could be playing for Barcelona! When did she get so good?"

"Olivia went to Everton Soccer Academy with me this summer," Sam said, walking by to get his water. He shook his head so that the rain and sweat fell down on Jax. "Be afraid. She's awesome. I bet she'll get tapped for the girls' Elite Team when she's old enough. She even got some shots past *me,* and we all know how hard that is!"

Jax pretended to vomit on the grass while Sam guzzled his water.

Henry spoke for the first time. He had been staring, mesmerized, at the field. Jax figured he was putting Eli's wisdom to work.

"She's . . . she's HOT!" he said finally. "Did you hang out with her, Sammy?

Sam snorted his water, and Jax felt like he was going to vomit for real.

"Seriously, Henry? Are you, like, feverish or something? We have a soccer game to play and a bunch of giant U-Twelve girls to beat! And she's older than you!" Jax was disgusted.

"Only by a year—big deal! Please, Sam?"

Once Sam had recovered, he threw a muddy arm over Henry's shoulder. "Sure, Hen. I can hook you up. Livie's pretty cool for a fifth grader."

They sauntered over to where the girls were lined up, alternating taking shots on their goalie, a tiny blond girl who looked like she couldn't reach anything but seemed to fly into the air and grab every ball that came her way. Jax trailed behind, confused.

"Hi, Olivia," Jax mumbled, still watching their goalie, who was saving everything. Henry started talking about soccer, trying to sound, Jax thought, like he knew everything about the sport. Livie giggled and glanced at her friend before answering. Sam was bouncing a ball on his foot. Three, four . . . He was up to thirty bounces before it fell. Jax felt even worse. He couldn't bounce it more than ten times before it went careening off. Mercifully, Coach Sean blew his whistle and called them in. Jax wasn't sure he could watch Henry trying to impress Sam—and Olivia—any longer.

"She's pretty cool, don't you think, J?" Henry asked. He walked a little faster than usual, his shoulders thrown back. Jax realized Henry had grown again. Now he was at least four inches taller than him. Jax sighed and hurried to keep up.

"Okay, U-Elevens, circle up!" Coach Sean yelled. "We're playing some older competition here, and, as some of you might know, my wife, Dennis's mom, coaches that team. His sister Caroline is the blond girl with orange cleats. We have a little wager on whose team will win, with the loser taking on dinner and cleanup for the next week. Now, as Dennis can tell you, it is not in anyone's best interest for me to lose! I'm counting on you."

Jax and his teammates looked at Dennis, one of the youngest players on the team, who was cackling maniacally at the thought of a grudge match between his parents. Then they looked across the field to the girls' team, where the coach, presumably Dennis's mom, was huddled up with the players.

"Eli, we're counting on your eyes here," Coach Sean continued. "As her father, it would be deeply unfair of me to tell you that Caroline can't shoot with her left foot, but if Eli happens to notice it, he should feel free to share. Okay. Everyone ready? Let's do it!"

Through this speech, Jax's eyes kept sliding to Henry, who in turn kept swiveling to stare at Olivia. When the two starting lineups hit the field, Jax couldn't help groaning. Henry was lined up against Livie.

"Henry!" Jax hissed right before the whistle blew. "Concentrate! This is *soccer*!"

Henry just glared at him, pushed his rain-soaked hair out of his eyes, and gave Olivia a dazzling smile—that she missed, because she had just taken a pass from her center and faked right past him.

Jax took off running. Between Sam's oh-so-helpful introduction and Eli's silent treatment, Jax was wishing he were an only child.

The girls' team won, 4–2, and it was time to go home, damp and dismal, in Dad's van. The smell of wet cleats was overpowering. Outside, it was almost dark, even though practices had been in full sunlight just a few short weeks before. Henry, who was getting a ride home, sat with Sam in the middle seats, laughing loudly and, Jax thought, stupidly, at every single thing Sam said. He didn't seem to even care that they'd lost. So what if it was only a scrimmage and didn't count? As far as Jax was concerned, it mattered.

Eli apparently felt Jax had been punished enough. "That was a tough one. Research has actually shown that girls mature faster than boys at this age, so for now they're stronger and taller. But in a year or two, that statistic will reverse. Even the most elite women athletes are at a huge disadvantage against male competitors."

Jax grunted. "It can't reverse soon enough for me. That was so lame. And how were people getting past that keeper? She could practically fly." He stared at Eli accusingly. Eli had whispered something to their teammates, and two of the boys had scored. But Jax, normally one of the top scorers, hadn't even gotten close.

Eli looked apologetic. "You just have to shoot low. She's so good at jumping—she used to be a gymnast—that she misses the ones rolling toward the low corners. That's where you needed to shoot."

Eli was silent for a minute. Jax thought about yelling at him for not telling him earlier, but decided not to. After all, the silent treatment was over. He sighed.

Eli said, "I should have told you. I'm sorry." He looked down at his muddy shin guards.

Jax shrugged, though the apology felt good. He smiled and reached out to punch Eli lightly on the arm.

"Yeah, you should have," he said. "That way we might have won. Poor Dennis!"

They both laughed. Coach Sean had told them that the week's menu was kielbasa sausage, fried SPAM, pancakes, and spaghetti.

"Yeah, and Coach Sean listed only four meals! What do you think he's going to do after that—repeat the whole batch?"

"Maybe he's going to start mixing and matching: spaghetti and SPAM, pancakes with kielbasa. . . ."

They were laughing so hard when the van stopped to drop Henry off that Jax almost forgot to say goodbye.

But at the last minute he yelled out the window, "Hey, H, I'll see you at school tomorrow, 'kay?"

"See you," Henry answered. "Hey, Sam, I'll see you there too. Can you tell me more about what you guys did at camp?"

Sam laughed. "Sure thing, H. See you tomorrow."

"See you tomorrow," Jax echoed. But he wasn't sure Henry heard.

Chapter Seven

IN WHICH FROG RIDES THE BUS

Thank yu papa i lov yu. Ldybg is hpy to
lov Frog

Frog usually felt that being the youngest of four worked out pretty well. He rarely got blamed for things, since someone older always "should have known better," and even when he had chores, it was a good bet that someone else had to do them with him. But every once in a while, he hated being the youngest.

"WHY can't I ride the school bus? The other boys rode it in kindergarten! I want to. Flare wants to. His paws get tired walking, because he's not used to pavement. Pleeeeeeeeeeeeeease?" Frog made the word last as long as he could, stopping only when he had to breathe.

Papa threw his hands up. "They only rode the bus because I was home with you. Why on earth would you want to be on a bus that contributes fossil fuels to the environment and smells like old barf, when you can walk or bike with me? I don't get it." He started to walk back toward his office and tripped over Sir Puggleton, who barked.

"And it's when this beast gets his exercise, when I walk you to school. You want to deprive him?" He pointed to Sir Puggleton, who had fallen back asleep on the hall rug. Dad said Sir Puggleton had MIR—Maximum Inconvenience Radar.

It was raining again, so hard that even Coach Nan had agreed that soccer practice was impractical. So all the Fletchers were home, and the house, while spacious, felt very crowded. Jax and Eli were playing Stratego on the coffee table, Eli leaning over to give Jax just enough advice that he wouldn't lose quite so quickly. Sam was playing *Rock Band,* crashing on his video drums in ever-louder crescendos.

Frog pressed forward. "But you can walk Sir Puggleton later. As a break. Eli says brains need oxygen during the day, and that's why we have recess or whatever they call it at his school. So you could walk Sir Puggleton as your re-cess!" He was dazzled with his problem-solving prowess, and smiled at Papa, showing off the gap from his missing front tooth.

Papa stared down at him and sighed. "Why do you want to, Froggie? I still don't get it."

"Lots of my friends ride the bus. Ladybug is on the bus, and she said if I ride it, we can sit together."

Papa took a deep breath and exhaled through his nose.

Any louder and it would have been a snort. "Jeremiah. Ladybug is . . ." He paused. "Remember how we couldn't meet her at your class's open house?"

"I told you, she was sick. She had a rash and was itchy and couldn't come to school all that week."

Over at the television, the drums stopped drumming. Eli and Jax peered up from their game. Frog ignored this attention.

Papa took another tack. "Isn't it funny that a boy named Frog met a girl named Ladybug? It's like something that could happen in a made-up story, don't you think?"

The living room got, if anything, quieter.

But Frog didn't notice. "I know! That's how I knew we'd be friends! And she has two moms, like I have two dads! And she has three sisters, like I have—"

"Three brothers. I know, I know." Papa looked discouraged.

"But back to the school bus . . . Pleeease, Papa? Can I just try it? I really, really want to! PLEEEEEEASE?"

Papa sighed again. His eyes swept across the room, where Sam had *re*started his drumming and Eli was doing a butt-shaking victory dance over his board game win. Jax was intently picking dirt out from between his toes, his knees up level with his eyes. Papa's gaze returned to Frog, who was staring up pleadingly at him.

Papa threw his arms up again. "We could have adopted one little girl! One girl! But no. We chose to start a zoo instead!"

No one paid any attention. He said this at least once a week.

"What friends are on it? *Other* than the elusive Ladybug?" he asked Frog.

Frog rattled off the names of several classmates. "So? Can I?"

"At least the barfing Noah's not on it," Jax muttered to Eli.

Papa finally stepped over Sir Puggleton and headed back toward his office. "If riding a rickety and smelly bus every day is preferable to my ambulatory company, then I guess it's fine. We'll try it until winter vacation, then see."

Frog flung his arms around Papa's retreating leg. "Thank you so much! I can't wait to tell Ladybug!"

"Sure, sure. Go tell her," Papa said, trying to beat a final retreat.

"Silly Papa! I can't tell her until I see her at school tomorrow." Frog didn't see his brothers rolling their eyes. "But she'll be so excited. I can't wait!"

The following Monday, Jax and Sam set off on foot as usual. Eli got in the car with Dad, also as usual. And Frog, officially approved for the bus, stood with Papa at the school bus stop down the street. There were around six other kids also waiting there, all kindergarten students like Frog. Two of them, Grace and Harry, ran over to Frog and hugged him.

"You're on the bus! You're on the bus!" Grace yelled.

Frog was so excited, he was bouncing from one foot to the other, his overlarge backpack swinging dangerously from side to side, threatening to topple him.

Frog loved his backpack. Sometimes he filled it with gravel from the driveway to make it as heavy as possible.

"Is this little one your only child?" a woman asked Papa as Frog swung around and around, causing the other children to move slightly closer to their parents.

"No," Papa answered heavily. "Frog's the youngest of four."

"Four! You must be keeping busy!" she answered. Then she added tentatively, "Is his name Frog? Like the animal?"

"Not exactly," Papa answered. Like introductions of their unconventional family, this was well-covered territory for Papa. "His real name is Jeremiah, but when he was just a little guy, his brothers used to sing the old song 'Joy to the World.' You know, 'Jeremiah was a bullfrog/ Was a good friend of mine'? Well, it didn't take long before he was being called Bullfrog more than Jeremiah by his brothers. And now he's just Frog."

To her credit, the woman looked pleased with the explanation, even though Frog had just crashed his backpack into her knees with a particularly violent bounce.

"It's coming! It's coming!" Frog shouted as the yellow bus pulled up to the curb, its red lights flashing festively.

He turned and gave Papa a huge hug. "I love you, Papa! Thank you SO much for letting me ride the bus! Ladybug and I will wave to you—look for us!"

Getting in line behind the other kids, Frog craned his neck, trying to look into the bus.

"Be careful!" Papa said. "And *listen to the grown-ups!* And maybe sit with— Oh, forget it!"

Papa gave up his warnings as the bus doors closed behind Frog. At least Frog seemed to be sitting next to a real child as the bus pulled away.

Chapter Eight

IN WHICH CAMPING AND COMPUTERS DON'T MIX

TO: LUCY_CUPCAKE
FROM: PAPABEAR
SUBJECT: Camping weekend
Hey, Luce—

Just thought you'd enjoy seeing a few photos of your nephews at the farm, especially the last one. I took it after a short but exciting rain shower. Jax and Sam decided to see if they could camouflage themselves so completely in mud that we couldn't find them in the field. It worked. We should have left them there. . . .

Love, Bro

"WE'RE ON THE WAY, WE'RE ON THE WAY, WE'RE ON THE WAY TO THE FARM!" Frog sang at the top of his lungs. They were all crammed into the van—Papa and Dad in the front, Eli and Sam in the middle (because of car sickness and family ranking, respectively), and Jax, Frog, and Sir Puggleton in the back. Behind them were the enormous tent, the six sleeping bags, twelve bags of groceries, and the multiple piles of gear required for the Fletchers to spend even three nights away from home.

Frog's brothers joined in with varying degrees of enthusiasm. The annual camping weekend in Maine was a sacred date on the Fletcher calendar, and despite having to miss soccer games and birthday parties, the family had kept the tradition for ten years. While some years it had rained so hard that they'd lasted only a night, and other years the nights had been so cold that they had woken up to frost on the tent, mostly the memories were of perfect fall evenings, a full orange moon rising over haystacks, and campfires that went long into the night. No one was willing to give it up.

Still, Eli thought, it wasn't quite the same from one year to the next. This year Sam was plugged into his music player, his head bobbing up and down to the loud and angry-sounding lyrics that came faintly through the earbuds. Jax was mad, sulking over an argument they'd been having, over whether Wolverine or Cyclops from X-Men would win in a fight. And . . . this was the part Eli didn't want to think about . . . he himself had brought a computer, against all Fletcher Family Rules. This was because his teacher had been unimpressed to hear he was missing school for this annual camping trip, and had stated that if Eli didn't log in his regular homework assignment on Monday (an assignment that wasn't posted until Friday, so he couldn't do it in advance), he would be docked a full grade. So Eli was lugging Papa's laptop, which had led to an avalanche of complaints, which in turn had led to Sam's asking if there was an Internet connection at the farm, which had then led to Papa's bellowing that no child of his was going to be texting and chatting online for the only seventy-two hours a year they were truly out in nature. The whole thing was a pain, Eli thought, and he couldn't help remembering Grove Lower Elementary, where the annual camping trip was a known entity to all the teachers, who enjoyed hearing about it but made it clear they would never go anywhere where they'd have to use an outhouse all weekend.

"Do you think there will be more kittens?" Jax asked, leaning over the back of Eli's seat.

"Of course. There are always more kittens. It's the farm!" Frog answered before Eli could say anything. "I wonder if the tiny gray one will still be there."

"Dummy! The tiny gray one won't be tiny anymore. He'll be grown up. He might be a mom now," Jax answered.

"That would be a dad, Jax," Dad said from the front seat. "And daddy cats are not really known for their parenting skills."

"Indeed!" said Papa. "Why, if it weren't for the hard

work of the mother cats, it would be a *cat*-astrophe!" He chortled, while half the car groaned and the other half ignored him, Eli included. It was better not to pay attention to Papa's puns.

"Whatever," Jax said, with a fine disregard for the logistics of cat family dynamics. "He'll be big and there will be more kittens, that's my point. And I wonder how many chickens they have this year. And maybe I can help milk the goats!"

"Sam, will you tell us stories in the tent again?" Frog asked. "Maybe another one about the two brother lions. I loved that one."

Sam turned around to smile at his littlest brother. "Sure, Froggie. Zacker and Whacker . . . remember? That's what I named them. I'll have to think of some good adventures for them." Sam forgot he was the oldest and coolest when they got to the farm.

The farm was a special place, open to campers only one weekend a year, when the nearby county fair was going on. The Fletchers had met Rob and Karen Bean, the owners, the first year the Beans had thought to let visitors camp in their back fields once the haying had been done, and the two families had been fast friends ever since.

The fair was fun too, but for Eli, at least, the best part was seeing the Bean kids. They were somewhere close in age to Jax and Sam—Eli could never remember exactly what their ages were—but since they were homeschooled, they were democratic about playing with all Fletcher boys equally. The younger one, Anna, had become a special friend and sometime pen pal of Eli's. Last year they had discussed the benefits of a yurt versus a tree house, and this time Eli had brought along a few library books on these two types of dwellings that he was sure she'd love.

The sky was already darkening as they jittered and jutted down the dirt driveway that led to the farm. As they emerged at the end, the car was immediately surrounded by barking dogs, chickens, and Bean children. Papa stepped on the brake.

"Okay, everyone but Dad, OUT! That includes Sir Puggleton!"

There was a wild scrum of bodies shoving toward the door at the same time, with, as usual, Frog getting squeezed to the back and tumbling out the rear hatch when someone finally opened it for Sir Puggleton.

"You know the rules," Papa called out the open window as he started driving carefully across the meadow to their camping spot. "Stay with at least one other person. Stay clear of the campfire. Don't kiss the chickens. . . ." His voice faded away.

Frog rolled his eyes. "I don't know why he has to say that. I only did it once!"

Sir Puggleton had a glorious reunion with the farm dogs, who immediately took him off to pee on some new bushes. The boys gazed with grins on their faces at the orange sunset blazing over the farm. Hugging his backpack to his chest, Eli stood next to Anna, who was now taller than him. He wondered if she had gotten all girly since last year.

"You're here!" she said with a huge smile. "Finally! I've been watching for you guys for an hour."

"Are there new kittens?" Frog asked, at the same time that Sam said, "Where's Ben? Did he get the dirt bike he was talking about?"

Anna answered them both. "Yes, and yes. Frog, the newest litter is only a few weeks old, so they're really shy. But if you're patient, up in the hayloft, they might peek out. There was another litter born back in July, and they're nuts. They're always climbing up your back, and they keep creeping into the tents of the campers who arrived yesterday. They're behind the milking barn. Ben's there too. He can tell you about the dumb bike—so far he's needed stitches twice."

She turned to Eli as the three other boys darted off. "How was your year? Thanks for sending those email links. The 3-D one of the yurt was awesome. Did you ever get to do a model of a suspension bridge over the summer? And did you see photos of that one in India? It's practically two thousand feet long. So cool!"

Eli grinned. This was the Anna he remembered. Grabbing the books from his backpack, they sat on one of the carved logs by the empty fire pit, which would be lighted later that night, and began to talk.

By the time the boys reunited at their campsite, the tent was up, Dad was laying out sleeping bags, and Papa was lighting their cooking fire. They would head up to the big campfire later in the evening for marshmallows and singing.

"So, guys, how is it? Any major changes?" Dad asked, his voice muffled from within the tent. The beam of his headlamp flashed around inside the blue walls.

"Not much," Sam answered. "We saw Rob, and he said he'd be down later to say hello, and that Karen will see us at the fire—she's crazy busy because they're entering chickens and goats in the fair this year. And of course her sewing stuff. Benji says she's been absolutely berserk for weeks now. He says they've been eating dinner at ten o'clock every night."

"Farming's not for the faint of heart," said Papa, snapping more kindling for the fire. "It's not like you can negotiate your deadlines. When you've got animals depending on you, and your living depending on those animals, it's three hundred sixty-five days a year. And speaking of deadlines, when do you want to get that assignment, Eli? Heaven forbid you delay one math worksheet—"

"Easy, Jason. Eli's just trying to be conscientious,"

Dad said from the tent. "Though it does seem a bit excessive to require you to lug a computer up here and do this when you'll only miss one full school day. Still, I guess that's the Pinnacle way!"

Eli didn't say anything. The computer felt like a huge heavy weight he had to carry around, refusing to let the farm work its usual magic on him. Dad and Papa had moved on to discussing how much ice they needed to keep the bacon cold, so Eli didn't bother to answer. Instead he moved closer to the fire, enjoying the heat and the flames as the evening's light disappeared and night fell.

The big bonfire that night was wonderful, huge and blazing in the darkness of the Maine night. The July kittens were as much of a menace as Anna had warned, pouncing on moths and chasing each other across the laps and heads of all the unsuspecting campers. Still, once they had used up their burst of energy, they collapsed in small purring heaps on whoever was closest. Eli cuddled a fiery orange one whose purr was almost loud enough to drown out the grown-ups' singing.

"So, I started a new school this year. I don't know if I told you," he said to Anna, who was holding an all-black kitten.

"Oh! Right. How is it?" Anna asked.

Eli sighed and held the orange kitten more tightly. The

thought of the computer in the back of the van felt once again like an ominous timer ticking away. But he had begged so hard to go to Pinnacle!

"It's cool. The kids are really smart, and my teacher is so tough. I mean . . ." He paused for a second. "Well, one cool thing is that we can do these weekly research projects on whatever we want, and if we're really interested, we can keep researching the same thing for three weeks!"

Anna looked confused. "Is that a special treat?" she asked.

"Well, in most schools you have to do whatever work the teacher tells you. And you might not be allowed to research something just because it's interesting."

"Not allowed to do research?" Anna laughed. "What do they do—punish you?"

Eli thought about how to explain it. "No, it's not like that. It's just . . . during a regular school day there might not be any time for something like researching what you want."

"But you can do it on your own, right? No one's going to stop you?"

"Yeah." Eli wasn't getting his point across. "But you don't get credit for it. It doesn't count." Even as he said it, he knew Anna was going to laugh, and he couldn't blame her.

"So let me get this straight," she said, giggling so hard, her kitten gave a disgruntled blatting sound and curled up more tightly under her chin. "You can learn whatever you want, whenever you want, but at your new school you get credit for it and at your old school you didn't?"

Eli nodded glumly. It did sound kind of stupid. He looked up from the fire, and saw his brothers—Frog curled up asleep on Dad's lap; Sam and Jax on either side of Ben, looking at a dirt bike magazine by the light of the fire; and Papa singing with Rob, Karen, and the rest of the grown-ups while a few of them played guitars. He vaguely recognized the song as one of Frog's lullabies.

He turned back to Anna, squeezing his kitten. "Truthfully, I don't like it all that much. We have to sit still practically all day. Instead of recess we get these really short 'oxygen breaks.' It's . . ." He looked down at the sleeping ball of fur. "It's just not that fun. And I never thought school was supposed to be fun, but now that it isn't . . ."

He stopped talking. He hadn't planned to tell anyone he didn't like his school, not even Anna. After all, he had begged to go there. He had gotten the application forms and told his parents about it and promised he would do anything they asked if only he could go. The Grove school had been pretty fun, but mostly it had been boring sitting around with his work finished way before anyone else. He had been sure the Pinnacle School was the right place. But now that he was there, he wasn't sure at all.

Chapter Nine

IN WHICH JAX TACKLES
(OR IS TACKLED BY) HALLOWEEN,
VETERANS, AND WET CATS

I am dropping off the three balls, two badminton birdies, and four pieces of crumpled construction paper that have all landed in my yard since the weekend. I believe I have made myself clear on the subject, but if not let me say it again: Keep your belongings on your property. The balls have damaged my autumn annuals and frightened my dog.

Further, I will request again that you refrain from making inappropriate amounts of noise. While the police did not seem concerned the last time I discussed it with them, they did tell me to remain in contact should there be further problems. Be sure that I will.

S. Nelson

"He's a freaking jerk. Seriously." Sam was breathing hard, still sweaty from practice. "Why does he have to be so up-tight?"

He threw his soccer ball on the floor and kicked off his cleats, nudging them in the direction of the coat closet.

"What the heck is wrong with him?" He brandished the note. "Blah, blah, blah 'keep your belongings on your property'! Blah, blah, blah 'will contact the police'! He stinks."

"What's going on?" Jax called. He was in the bath-tub. The downstairs bathroom was conveniently located off the family room, so he could keep track of everything happening, making it more interesting than using the bathroom near their bedrooms. His own practice had ended an hour ago, and Papa had threatened to withhold dinner until he was clean.

"Mr. Nelson left another nasty note on the door. It must have been after you got home," Dad said. He helped coach Sam's team, and he was almost as sweaty as Sam. Dropping his soccer bag by the door, Dad stuck his head into the bathroom to say hello to Jax. His glasses steamed up in the hot room, and he beat a hasty retreat.

"Did he at least return the orange ball?" Jax asked.

"Of course not. I haven't seen it since the first day of school. It's probably jammed in the hedge or something and he's too lazy to get it out. He really is lame," Sam said.

He returned from the kitchen and leaned against the

bathroom doorway, looking slightly more cheerful now that he had a cookie safely in his hand and another in his mouth.

"It's true," Sam said, somewhat indistinctly, around the mouthful of cookie. "I mean, what's his problem? He lives in a neighborhood with kids. What does he expect?"

"Maybe he's like the Grinch, and his heart is two sizes too small," piped up Frog from the couch, where he was driving his race car across Sir Puggleton's back.

Sam just snorted. "Whatever. He has a nice house. He's healthy enough to be outside messing around in his stupid garden every day. What's his problem?"

Jax ignored his brother and dunked underwater. He needed to think. He had to turn in the first piece of his Veteran Project tomorrow, and he still had no idea who he was interviewing. This step was pretty easy; he just needed a name and what war it was. Then his parents had to sign the paper. It shouldn't be a big deal. Henry had some second cousin who had served in Iraq and now lived in Boston. But Jax had no one. And the secret truth was, he really wanted to talk to a veteran. Even though he had never known them, the adoption agency had told his dads that Jax's biological parents had both been in the army. He couldn't help wondering what it would be like to interview *them* for this project. Blowing bubbles, he surfaced with a loud splash. That was stupid to even think about, since he didn't have the faintest clue who they were. He just needed to find any veteran—and fast. And preferably someone cool who had done awesome stuff and who Jax could interview and get his project in the paper.

The fall was moving more quickly than usual, maybe because the weather was so perfect that all the boys stayed outside until the very last minute of sunlight. But the last minute was coming earlier and earlier. The days were getting shorter, the bright red and orange and yellow leaves had started turning a boring brown and dropping in huge numbers, and—most exciting of all—Halloween was only a week away.

Jax decided to ignore the matter of the Veteran Project for a few more minutes and focus on the even more important deadline: Halloween. The Fletchers threw an annual night-before-Halloween party, and this year would be epic.

"So we're definitely doing the haunted yard, not just inside the house, right, Dad? Right? We'll have to start setting it up this weekend. We've never had it outdoors before. It should be sick. I still can't decide what to be. I'm thinking about being ectoplasmic slime. Or a Gryffindor Quidditch player. I wanted to do something together with Henry, but he's being a nimrod."

He splashed some more, this time in irritation. Jax tried not think about the past few weeks at school—Henry wearing some weird super-dark jeans instead of his normal sports pants, listening to rap on his iPod before school, bobbing his head to the music like he thought he looked cool.

"Why? What's going on with the Hen?" asked Dad from the couch, where he had begun correcting history papers. "Ugh! Why me? Why? How can my students confuse Little Rock and Plymouth Rock?"

Jax ignored him. Dad was usually quite calm, but his students' mistakes could send him into a frenzy.

"Henry's in loooooooove," answered Sam. He leaned against the bathroom door, holding a huge sandwich. Dinner was cooking, but no one worried about Sam losing his appetite. It was, as Eli had once said, a statistical impossibility. "He follows Olivia Grayson around like a puppy. She thinks it's cute."

Jax gave a particularly ferocious splash. "He's being a moron! And he wants to go as some sparkly vampire because he says girls love sparkly vampires."

He forced himself to calm down. Maybe all Henry needed was a sick Halloween party to remind him how much fun they used to have. "Now, Sam, you're being the Grim Reaper, right? And you'll be really spooky. And Eli— AAAAAAAAHHHHHHHHHHHHHHHHHHHHHH!"

There was a loud splash and a clattering scuffling sound, and Jax shrieking in pain. Seconds later, Zeus, the seventeen-pound Maine coon cat, raced out of the bathroom, soaking wet and hissing at everything in his path.

"What the—" Dad yelled, his papers flying everywhere

as the dripping cat leaped onto the couch and then over it back to the floor.

Sam flung his sandwich into the air in surprise. "Somebody catch the cat before he goes to Papa's office! He's on a video call with India!"

Everyone moved at once. Sir Puggleton leaped into action, darting around the cat to try to get to the sandwich, while Sam fought to get past the dog and to the office door. Eli and Frog, unencumbered by a hungry dog, dashed off to try to catch Zeus. Dad went to check on Jax.

Jax was rattled. "Look at me. LOOK at me!" he shouted. "I'm bleeding in ten different spots. It's not relaxing at all, I can tell you, having that fifty-pound monster with twenty claws coming flying in at you!"

The bathwater was considerably lower now, the bulk of it on the floor or, indeed, still being dripped around the house by a frantically angry Zeus.

Jax could tell Dad was trying hard not to laugh. "What happened?" Dad asked.

"That *stupid* cat just fell in, that's what happened! He was doing that thing he does—you know, when he wants to drink from the bathtub. He had his head down really low, and I just moved a tiny bit, but I guess it freaked him out or something, because he gave this crazy jump, and the next thing I knew, there was wet fur and hissing and so many claws! I swear he has, like, fifty claws! It was awful!"

But before Dad could answer, they both heard Papa approaching.

"Can someone tell me," he began, clutching the hissing, dripping Zeus firmly, "why it is that my employees in Bangalore, India, were treated to the sight of this"—he held out the soaked cat—"racing over my desk, followed by two of our sons? One of whom was wearing nothing but his underwear and a cape?"

He paused, still holding the dripping cat. Jax forgot his wounds and tried not to giggle at the sight of Zeus, small and pathetic with his massive bushy coat matted down, and Papa's ferocious scowl.

Papa went on. "I work from home, you realize, with the communal understanding that my office is a fortress never, ever to be breached, except in case of fire or burglars. Of course, that rule would be easier to enforce if the darn door would stay shut. But this"—he held out and shook the wet cat—"is neither a fire nor a thief. So why was it in my office?

"I believe I might have frightened my employees into fits. In fact, they may be filing a lawsuit against me as we speak. Tom," he continued, "help me. Tell me there's a way to explain this."

At this, Dad lost his battle with laughter. He sat down on the toilet and laughed until he cried.

Jax was deeply glad Henry didn't need to know about this most recent episode of Fletcher life. If he was trying to be cool these days, a naked bleeding friend, a soaking cat, and a hysterical father were the last things Jax wanted to share.

. . .

It wasn't until after he had applied Band-Aids and gotten dressed that Jax remembered the Veteran Project. He brought it up as they were serving themselves dinner.

"I need to find a veteran," he said, helping himself to chicken tikka masala. "Tonight. The project sheet is due tomorrow."

"Walk us through the timing of this, Jax," Dad said. "I'm a little concerned to hear that you have something due tomorrow and we didn't know about it."

"It's just the initial planning sheet," Jax said. "I'll show you the timeline after dinner. But basically I just need a name and a war. Then I start my research at school in the computer lab. We collect information and work on the historical—what's the word? Oh, yeah—context. We work on the historical context at school. Ms. Sugarman says it's so we don't sound like a bunch of dunderheads when we do our interviews, which doesn't happen until after winter break." He broke off to shove down a huge bite of naan, the Indian bread he loved.

"Anyway, right now I just need a name," he said indistinctly. "I don't have to do anything else."

"There's always Mr. Nelson," Eli said. "At least he lives nearby."

"And he's pretty old. He might have fought in a cool war," Sam added.

Papa looked like he was about to ask which wars were

the cool ones, but Jax cut him off with a groan. "But he's so mean! And he hates us."

"He fought in the Vietnam War, remember?" Eli said. "He has a bumper sticker."

"He doesn't hate us," Dad said. "But it's true you'll have to try to improve neighborly relations before you can interview him. That's called diplomacy. It's when one country tries to work things out by using discussions rather than force. The Fletcher-Nelson border conflicts could use some diplomacy. It's not such a bad idea, J-man. Think about it. Maybe you can get to know him a bit."

"It would be kind of interesting," Eli said, his eyes brightening. "Just, you know, as an experiment. Scientifically speaking, what happens when kindness is applied to a grouchy neighbor?"

Frog looked curious. "What kinds of things would you do?" he asked. "Would you invite him to play games and stuff? Or maybe he'd want to come over and help make cookies sometime. Katie lives on the other side of us, and she makes cookies with us, and she likes us, so maybe that would work."

Jax glanced at Dad, imagining Frog racing over and inviting Mr. Nelson to play Connect Four. That was *not* what this project needed. He just needed a veteran to interview.

"Let's not get too enthusiastic, okay, Froggie? Maybe

let Jax do it, so we don't overwhelm Mr. Nelson," Dad said.

Jax shrugged. "I'm game to try it," he said. "It's not like I have any other ideas." Diplomacy sounded cool. And Mr. Nelson was so grouchy, he was kind of mysterious. Maybe he had done something really awesome, something that would get Jax into the newspaper.

"Do you need to get his signature?" Papa asked. "Maybe you should ask him before assuming he'll do it."

Jax paused, then shook his head. "Nah, it doesn't say anything about the veteran signing. And I'll only need to interview him for, like, an hour sometime this winter. It'll be fine."

He paused for a minute. "It might be better to start the diplomacy *after* Halloween. I'm not sure he's going to be crazy about our party, but I guess we can invite him. And speaking of Halloween—"

Sam, Eli, and Frog all started talking at once about special effects and costumes, and Jax almost—but not quite—managed to forget he had just agreed to interview Mr. Nelson.

Chapter Ten

IN WHICH THE HALLOWEEN PARTY ARRIVES AND NEARLY FLOATS AWAY

You're Invited! Have a Howling Good Time
for Halloween!
  WHEN: Friday, October 30, 6:00 p.m.
  WHERE: The Fletcher backyard
(It's outdoors this year, so dress warmly.)
  WHY: It's Howl-o-ween!
(And you can still trick-or-treat the next day.)
                  Hope you can join us!
                  —Jax and the Fletchers

This outdoor party was definitely more work than anyone had planned, Eli thought. It had all the usual parts of the Fletcher Halloween party, with Eli and Papa working on light and sound effects, Sam and Dad setting up joke-store skeletons on old furniture, and Frog working on a variety of disgusting Touch and Guess buckets that ranged from gummy worm "intestines" in cooking oil to sea sponge "brains" pickled in vinegar. Eli tried to keep his distance from Frog's experiments. But now there were more spaces to fill, more games to create, and, of course, there was more noise.

Papa had rigged up speakers, and songs like "Werewolf of London" came blasting out at intervals as he checked wiring and sound. Mr. Nelson had been coming out and staring from his porch, shaking his head in clear disapproval. He did *not* look impressed. Eli thought of Jax's project and sighed. Eli should at least say hi. Maybe if he didn't assume the worst about Mr. Nelson, it would go better. Cautiously optimistic, he walked over to the low bushes that separated their yards. But before he could say a word, Mr. Nelson started talking.

He didn't even start with hello.

"Let me tell you right now, I don't like the look of this. I thought this was a 'quiet residential neighborhood,' according to that real estate lady. What's all this?"

"It's our Halloween party," Eli said, trying to sound accommodating. "I think my brother Jax asked you to join—" Unfortunately, Papa chose that moment to blast the heavy metal song "Welcome to the Jungle" from the loudspeakers. Eli winced.

Mr. Nelson did not look happy. "What the heck do you need a party for? Isn't it enough to go around begging for candy like everyone else?"

Eli was sure he was the kind of neighbor who would keep his porch light off to discourage trick-or-treaters. Figured.

"Well, Jax had an idea—" Eli started.

"Which one is that?" Mr. Nelson interrupted. "The black one? Or the teeny little brown one?"

Eli sighed. "Jax is ten, Mr. Nelson. He's African-American. Frog is Indian, and he's si—"

Mr. Nelson interrupted again. "Well, whichever he is, I don't know why he'd need a party. But I'll tell you this: It better be quiet here by eight. On the dot. Or tell your father he'll be hearing from me!"

Eli stared after him a moment, and sighed. "Come by if you want!" he called. But he knew it was pointless.

Jax had finally decided to be a ninja, but because Dad wouldn't let him trick-or-treat the next day in all black (car dangers), he decided to be an intergalactic ninja, who had to wear all orange to blend in with the sun. Certainly no one could miss him now—he looked like a somewhat dangerous traffic cone. Frog was going as Zacker, the smaller—and smarter—of the lion brothers in Sam's stories. Unfortunately, many people confused Zacker with Flare, causing Frog to roll his eyes and say, "Silly! Zacker is made up."

Eli was going as Zeus (the god, not the cat), and had

made a bolt of lightning that could light up when he pressed it. And Sam was the Grim Reaper—Death himself—with a menacing face and an empty gaze he'd been practicing in the mirror all week.

"Sam, you should tell ghost stories!" Jax said, walking by with a screwdriver for Dad. "You'd look sick. Frog got scared when you made those dinosaurs come to life and fight Zacker and Whacker, and you looked normal then. He'd freak out if you looked like that!"

"Sam, can you stop clenching your jaw and bring me an extension cord? NOW!" Papa roared from across the yard. He was working to set up the crowning glory of the yard, the black bouncy castle.

"How this went from a simple trick-or-treat occasion to something that rivals a wedding in cost and time is a true mystery," he mumbled, holding one edge of the tarp in his mouth.

Eli walked toward them, pressing the button on his lightning bolt. It worked beautifully, most of the time. He looked up uneasily as a new wave of brown leaves came raining down on them in the stiff wind.

"Have you checked the weather?" he asked.

"As of this morning it was supposed to be cloudy with showers after midnight," came Papa's voice from behind the massive black plastic. "Ah, here we go. Get ready for a noise!"

And with a huge humming buzz, the generator began

inflating the castle. In the gloom of the cloudy afternoon it looked perfect.

"Costume time!" said Jax. He was nearly vibrating with excitement, his hair brushed straight out into what Sam called his Fletch-fro—a Fletcher Afro. Why an intergalactic ninja would have hair that stood out was unclear, unless he'd gotten electrocuted by the sun, thought Eli. But he didn't say anything to Jax. He watched Sam paint his face a gaunt and pallid white, then use a black grease crayon to draw hollows under his eyes and below his cheekbones. He looked horrible and ghostly. It was awesome.

Dad peered into the bathroom, where they were getting ready. "All set? People should be coming any minute." He was dressed in his usual history teacher garb, except he had a fake ax buried in his head, complete with blood and brains spilling down the back of his shirt.

"How do I look?" Dad asked. "I'm calling my costume 'the C-student's revenge.' Do you like it?"

Jax tentatively touched the goop on his dad's back. "SICK! Really nasty! What is it?" he asked.

"Cottage cheese mixed with a little black food coloring. Nice, eh?" Dad looked pleased with himself.

Eli looked in the mirror. His Greek chiton, or toga, was knotted perfectly (even if he had to wear his gray long underwear underneath to keep warm), and his long white beard and hair made him look ancient and wise. He clutched his electronic lightning bolt and hurried into the yard, where the first few kids were wandering up the driveway through the darkening twilight. The yard looked just perfect in this light, he thought. The torches blazed along the back fence, and in the shadows of the neighbors' massive trees, the whole place was spookier than he could have imagined a few hours ago, when Dad had been madly stapling fabric over the swing set to make a demon's cave and Papa had been swearing at the bouncy house, which had blown a fuse three separate times, and deflated like the world's most depressed balloon each time. But now it was as scary and wonderful as Eli could have hoped.

Jax ran by, chasing Henry, who was wearing a long black cloak and had his face painted pale, with his hair slicked back and tiny fangs protruding from his mouth.

"C'mon, Hen. Let's get in the bouncy house!" Jax was pleading, but Henry shook his head.

"No can do. It'th almotht impothible to thpeak with the fangth. If I jump, I'll probably kill mythelf!"

Jax looked disgusted, but Eli couldn't help laughing. Papa walked by, his pirate wig tilted slightly on his head. He grinned at Eli.

"This is pretty cool, E-man. The outdoor party might be the best one yet!"

Eli had to agree.

. . .

There are at least fifty people here, Eli thought, and more were walking in, toward the loud music and cheerful voices.

"Did you hear back from anyone at Pinnacle?" Papa asked, walking by with his arms full of juice boxes.

"Well, Ambrose is planning to try to come, even though it's a long drive for him. Most people don't live that close, really," Eli said.

"Your Shipton pals are here, though. I saw Jamil—I assume he's a Jedi, but I wasn't sure which one. It's good to see him and the rest of the old gang, right?" Papa said, carefully dropping the juice boxes into a large cooler filled with ice.

"Yeah, it's awesome to see them," Eli said. He sounded glum, even to himself. The problem wasn't seeing his friends; it was how much he missed them these days. But before Papa could react, Eli looked up.

"Um . . . is that—" Before he could get the question out, it was answered. The flash of light was indeed real lightning, far more impressive than the wired bolt he was carrying. And seconds later the slow, rumbling thrum of thunder came rolling across the yard.

"No. Ohhhhhhhh, no, no, no. This can't happen. It's not supposed to rain until after midnight," said Papa in a hushed, stricken voice.

But no one had told the rain. The first heavy drops started to splat loudly on costumes, props, and the bouncy house.

"Jason! Unplug the castle! Quick!" Dad's voice came through the darkness. "Okay, everyone out of the bouncy house! Sorry, guys—too dangerous! Everyone out!"

Seconds later the noisy generator was off, and the slow hiss of the escaping air filled the sudden silence.

For a few minutes it seemed like the rain was only teasing them, and everyone milled around, trying gamely to enjoy the spooky effects. Eli decided it was safe to demonstrate his lightning bolt again, and started fake zapping Jamil and Miles, who both swung their light sabers back at him. The music seemed especially loud, with the rattle of the generator gone.

Eli was mid-bolt when he saw Mr. Nelson charging toward him through the crowd. Maybe he had actually taken them up on the invitation? It seemed unlikely. Eli grimaced and looked around quickly to see if Dad or Papa was nearby. But he was the only Fletcher in the vicinity.

Mr. Nelson pushed through the group of costumed friends and put his face close to Eli's. Eli wished he had worn a costume with a mask.

"Hi, Mr. Nelson," he said, raising his voice to be heard over the howling of "The Time Warp" on the speakers. "Um—happy Halloween. Do you want to see my lightning bolt?"

Mr. Nelson opened his mouth to answer, and suddenly a clap of thunder, so loud that Eli felt it in his feet, jarred the ground and caused some of the younger kids to scream.

Seconds later, the deluge began.

Mr. Nelson's eyes bulged, and he stared up at the sky as though he couldn't believe how wet he was getting.

"Do you want me to get an umbrella or something?" Eli asked. Somehow he doubted Mr. Nelson was going to stick around.

"Turn. Off. The. Music!" Mr. Nelson bellowed. He turned back toward his house. "Before I call the cops again!"

Eli glanced around. Mercifully, Papa was unplugging the speakers even as Mr. Nelson was slamming his door.

But what about the party? Everyone was wandering around, trying to find cover as best they could.

"Should we just head out, Jason?" asked Tyler's mom, Jenny. She was dressed as Professor McGonagall, her witch's hat drooping in the downpour.

"No! Of course not! We'll just . . . Maybe . . . I don't know," said Papa helplessly.

Eli was debating darting inside, when he heard Dad's voice above the increasingly loud babble of voices and rain.

Dad clapped his hands several times and then put his fingers into his mouth and whistled, a shrill, loud sound.

"Okay, ghouls and gals, listen up! Everyone march into

the garage, double time, where Sam will entertain every-one, young and old, with some great ghost stories. If you can give us a few minutes, we'll get the party organized and move inside."

The next flash of lightning was so bright that the whole scene was illuminated like someone had turned on a spot-light. Before the thunder could crash, everyone pushed to-ward the garage. The only one not running was Sam, who was standing dead still in the middle of the yard, glaring at his father. The look on his face, combined with his ter-rifying costume, actually made Eli shiver.

"What?" Sam was hissing to Dad, grabbing him by the shirttail. "I don't want to stand in front of all those people and tell stories! Why did you do that?"

Dad jerked free. "Sam, just deal with it! You tell sto-ries all the time when we're camping. I need someone old enough to keep an eye on the little kids—the parents are going to have to help us move all this stuff. Now GO!" He moved off toward the snack table.

The last thing Eli saw as he rushed toward the garage door, his toga drooping, was Dad's ax flying off his head as he ran to grab as many bowls as he could carry.

Inside the garage, almost sixty people stood, dripping and panting, and—each and every one—staring at Sam. Sam stared back.

"Uhhhhhhh," he said, and Josh, who was dressed as someone from an old horror movie, with a hockey mask over his face, began to snicker. Henry, his fangs dangling from one side, laughed too.

One of the younger kids from down the street yelled, "Are you going to tell us stories?"

"Yeah!" another called. "Scary ones! But not too scary."

Sam just stared out at them. Under the bright fluorescent lights of the garage, he looked like a drippy, nervous, middle school kid.

Another massive flash of lightning slashed outside the garage window. Then, with another crash of thunder even louder than the last, the lights went out. Everyone screamed.

"Don't panic! Nobody panic! It's just the lights!" Sam shouted.

Eli had an idea. He hopped up from where he was perched on the hood of the van and ran over to the wall. After squeezing between three kids, two dressed as farmers and one as a very damp cat, Eli sidled up to Sam.

"Here," he said quickly, handing Sam a flashlight. "Put it in your sleeve and hold it below your face, like this." He held it up, through the fabric, right under Sam's chin. The effect was chilling. Immediately the crowd quieted down, and a hush fell over the garage. The thunder crashed.

"Tell the one that Ben told us at the farm. . . . You know, about the man killed by the horse whose ghost haunted the barn. Only make it a car crash, right here in town, and have him haunt our garage," Eli whispered. "In fact, make it one of the first automobiles ever used in town, in 1909. Start by saying, 'I bet most of you didn't know that the former owners of this house owned one of the first automobiles in town. . . .' Go on! Do it!"

Sam cleared his throat. Eli was sure Sam knew that story; Frog had retold it ten times that day, and then had refused to go into the tent until Sam had told him a sappy Zacker and Whacker See a Rainbow story to calm him down.

"Good evening," Sam said slowly. "I suspect many of you don't know that on this very site, more than a hundred years ago . . ."

Eli smiled and climbed back onto the hood.

Long before the audience was tired of the stories, Dad and Papa came to call everyone into the house. Eli and Sam were the last to leave the garage.

"Thanks, E-man. You saved my butt," Sam said, his voice hoarse from all the talking, his eyes bright.

Eli grinned. Ambrose had slipped in during the story of the escaped murderer who had been caught just up the street. His eyes had widened at the story, and he had groaned the loudest when Dad had told Sam to wrap it up.

"You're really scary tonight! Really, really scary," Eli said.

Sam smiled even wider, and Eli felt great. It had been just the right thing to say.

Chapter Eleven

A BRIEF INTERRUPTION

THE *SAILOR'S LOG*
   Shipton's Oldest Newspaper
LOCAL SPOTLIGHT: FAMILY TRADITIONS,
   page 4, column B (part of a continuing series)
Interview by Julia Kirby, eighth-grade student at
   Shipton Middle School

Today I, as the student reporter for the *Sailor's Log,*
am interviewing a Shipton family, the Fletchers. Jason
Fletcher and Tom Anderson moved to town thirteen
years ago, and adopted four boys. Sam is twelve; Jax
is ten; Eli is also ten but is younger than Jax (according to Jax); and Jeremiah, who is called Frog, is six.
We are talking about family traditions, specifically
their annual Halloween party. This year their party got
extra attention when a tree down the street got struck
by lightning and the power in the neighborhood went
out for twelve hours. This reporter goes to the party
every year, since she lives on the next block, and in

her opinion, it was the best party ever! I am interviewing all six of the Fletchers in their home in Shipton. Also present are the family cat, named Zeus, and the family dog, named Sir Puggleton. Frog Fletcher would like me to note that Flare, a cheetah who remains invisible, is also here.

THE SAILOR'S LOG: First, what made you decide to move to Shipton?

JASON: The beach. Well, more precisely, the beach in November. If we had known what it was like crawling with tourists in August, we might have changed our minds!

TOM: We drove up here on a whim, looking for a place close enough to the regional high school to be an easy commute, but far enough away to feel like the country. Shipton was perfect. It's wonderful this time of year, with all the balsam wrapped around the lampposts and Santa arriving by boat in the harbor. It's a great place to raise a family.

JASON: If you don't go downtown or to the beach in the summer.

SL: You have a lot of boys. A *lot* of boys. How did you decide to adopt so many of them?

TOM: Yes, our boys are something else. We adopted Sam as an infant. He became our son hours after he was born, and his mother, whom I used to work with, is still in our life, though she moved to California. We knew we wanted a sibling for Sam, and the adoption lawyer told us there were two boys, almost the same age, who had become incredibly close in foster care. They were both a year old.

SL: Jax and Eli?

TOM: We had no intention of adopting two more.

JASON: Never let them outnumber you! That was my philosophy. Man-on-man defense all the way.

TOM: But once we met the two of them, Eli's tiny blond head bobbing around, following Jax everywhere he went ... well, it was a done deal.

JASON: So we went to zone defense. It's been painful. But once they outnumbered us, well, Frog just kind of felt like a rounding error. What's one more?

TOM: Very funny. Again, we had a connection to the family, this time through someone Jason worked with in Bangalore, India. Frog had some fairly serious medical issues that needed attention right at birth, and it was clear his mother would not be able to keep him. There was an enormous amount of paperwork, but ... Jeremiah, as we called him then, joined us when he was around three months old.

SL: Wow. That's a lot of boys.

FROG: Flare's a boy too.

ELI: All our pets are male! Zeus and Sir Puggleton are, at least, although I don't know about the fish we had.

JAX: But the fish died over summer vacation anyway, so it doesn't really matter.

FROG: Zeus and Sir Puggleton are kind of old and boring. We need to get a new pet, I think. Don't you think we should get a kitten?

[This reporter notes that both parents pretended not to hear the question, though it was repeated three times.]

SL: Right. So, this interview is about holiday traditions. Can you tell me what the traditions are in your house and why you have such a big Halloween party?

JASON: Ha!

TOM: Yes, well . . . believe it or not, it started with religion. We incorporate a lot of different religious traditions into our family. I was raised Episcopalian.

JASON: And I grew up Jewish—bar mitzvahed and everything.

TOM: And as the parents of an African American boy, we want to make sure Jax has his own history and cultural traditions recognized.

JASON: Then there's the fact that Frog was of course born into a Hindu family, so we can't leave him out.

SL: But what does all that have to do with Halloween?

TOM: Nothing!

JASON: That's just it. We wanted something that belonged to everyone in the family. Halloween is perfect. It's the celebration of old traditions and new ones.

TOM: For instance, did you know that it originated as an ancient druid celebration sometime around 700 B.C.? And that the tradition of jack-o'-lanterns began in Ireland, with carved turnips, as a way of scaring off evil spirits?

SAM: Dad, stop it. Seriously.

TOM: Sorry, I get carried away. But the point is that it's a really interesting holiday.

JAX: It's the candy holiday! It's awesome. It was my idea to have the outdoor party this year. It was really cool until the lightning.

SL: It *was* really cool. Moving on, do you celebrate other big holidays in your family?

TOM: We try to bring traditions together that honor the cultures our boys were born into, as well as our own families. So when we get to the winter solstice, that means lighting the Chanukah candles as well as the Kwanzaa candles, and it means making Christmas cookies and having a tree, but also celebrating the Hindu festival of Pancha Ganapati. It's a wonderful excuse to learn about and celebrate many cultures.

JASON: And it means the kids get a zillion presents. So they're on board.

JAX: Yeah, we get tons of presents. But it also means we have to write a zillion thank-you notes, and I hate writing. Oops, not newspaper writing, though. That would be cool.

TOM: Yes, from where they sit, the best part of being a

Fletcher is the number of days that involve presents, sweets, or celebrations. It's a good life.

SL: Wow, you guys are really lucky. And it's neat that you chose Shipton. I can't wait until next year's Halloween party.

JASON: Let's hope the power stays on.

Chapter Twelve

IN WHICH SAM THINKS HARD (AND NO, IT DOESN'T HURT)

Mr. Nelson,

We're so sorry that you were without power. However, I don't believe our bouncy castle and lights caused a power outage. The whole neighborhood was out, presumably because lightning hit a tree and knocked down the power lines.

Mr. Nelson, with all due respect, I don't think we are going to cancel Halloween next year in order to "avoid more trouble" from our "insane shenanigans," as you so eloquently put it. However, as a gesture of goodwill I am leaving three brand-new flashlights, and batteries, with this note. Hopefully it will help in the case of another power outage.

Sincerely and with all good neighborly wishes,

Tom Anderson

The week after Halloween was easily one of the best Sam had ever had. Well, other than Jax's failure to get even slightly on Mr. Nelson's good side. While the police had not shown up during the party, the three flashlights they had thoughtfully left for Mr. Nelson had been found, apparently flung with great force, in the Fletcher yard. But Sam couldn't worry about that. After the Halloween storm, the weather turned fall-perfect—chilly and sunny and just right for soccer games, apple cider, and biking or strutting to school with only a hoodie on. And strutting was what he was doing. Every kid in the neighborhood was running up to tell Sam how awesome his stories had been, begging for more.

"Come on. Can't you come over after school? I told Olivia and Alex and all those guys that I'd ask you. We can go down into our basement room," Nolan asked as they walked.

"Sorry, man," Sam answered, flattered beyond belief. "I have soccer."

Nolan looked disappointed. He was in sixth grade too, and lived around the corner, but since he played lacrosse and football, Sam rarely hung out with him. This was the first time Sam remembered ever being invited to his house.

"Well, can you at least tell how the story of the bloody hand ends? I heard you telling it at lunch yesterday, but the bell rang before you were done," Nolan pressed, clearly unwilling to give up.

Sam smiled and began.

• • •

As November continued, the weather turned less perfect, and a chilly drizzle fell for two weeks straight. The hoodie gave way to a Windbreaker and, finally, a ski jacket, but Sam's mood didn't fade with the fall sunshine. His stories sounded even better in the damp and drear, and he had been asked to tell funny Zacker and Wacker stories at Frog's friend's birthday party. Katie lived right next door, and her parents had even asked if they could pay him, which was unbelievably excellent. Of course, before Sam had been able to stammer out an answer, Papa had laughed and said they could pay him in cake. Not that Sam would have asked for money anyway, but it was so freaking cool that they'd offered.

It was only a few days before Thanksgiving when the signs went up around the Grove school.

AUDITION!!!!

BE A STAR AND SHINE ON THE GROVE SCHOOL'S STAGE!!

The posters listed the time and format of the play try-outs. Everyone, whether they wanted to be the star or just in the chorus, had to come prepared to sing a song, recite a short poem or story, and do something physical—a dance, a yo-yo trick, anything. Sam didn't even pause the first time he saw the sign. Plays had nothing to do with him. He was a soccer player, a pond-hockey guy, a ghost-story teller, not an actor. But then Ms. Daly pulled him aside after class.

"Sam, can you stick around for a minute?" she asked.

Sam stuck his hands deep into his pockets and shuffled over to her desk while she handed out lunch tickets. He knew what this was about. He and Tyler had gotten in trouble earlier for passing notes. But why was he the only one being asked to stay after class?

When Ms. Daly turned to face him, though, she was smiling. "I've heard from two lunchroom monitors that lunch has been much quieter, cleaner, and less crazy than usual because of a certain storyteller who has everyone totally wrapped up in his grisly tales," she said, laughing a little at the surprised look on his face. "In fact, one of them joked that she was going to ask me to extend your lunch period so she could hear how the story ended!"

Sam had to fight to keep from laughing out loud. Seriously? *This* was what he was being asked to stay for?

"Um, yeah," he mumbled, trying not to sound too proud. "I started telling some ghost stories at our Halloween party, and people really liked them."

Ms. Daly nodded. "I know. And that's what I wanted to talk to you about. I'm the director of the Grove school play. Maybe you saw the signs?"

Sam nodded, but he wasn't sure where she was going with this. She had to know he wasn't about to—

"I wondered if you'd be interested in auditioning," she

said, interrupting his thoughts with exactly the thing he was sure she wouldn't ask.

She must have been joking—he'd never acted in his life. Not that there was anything wrong with it, but he wasn't that type of kid. He was the play-sports-every-recess type, the make-the-A-team-in-soccer type, the can't-wait-for-the-high-school-ski-team type. *Not* the sing-and-dance-onstage type. Obviously.

He smiled and shook his head. "I don't think so," he said. "I'm not really into plays."

Her face fell a little. "Oh. That's too bad. You have a real gift for holding the audience's attention. And it's a blast. . . ." Her voice trailed off. "But if you're not interested, so be it. Too bad, though. We're going to try to go into Boston to see Blue Man Group and eat in China-town . . . but no worries. You'd better head off to lunch!"

She gave him a smile before she turned back to her desk, but Sam could see he had disappointed her.

He stayed still for a moment longer, until she looked up at him with a puzzled smile.

"Well, I'm really busy," he said. But she didn't say anything else, just looked at him. He shrugged. "What's the practice schedule like?" he asked.

She smiled like he had just said something brilliant. "It's rehearsals, actually, not practice. But here." She pulled a piece of paper off her desk. "That should give you an idea of the time commitment."

Sam glanced down at the paper, then looked more closely. Was she nuts? There were practices three nights a week starting after winter break. There was no way to do that and play indoor soccer. And the way Coach Javi felt about commitment . . . Sam knew there was no choice. He dropped the sheet back onto her desk.

"Sorry. I don't think so," he mumbled. He walked away so he wouldn't see the disappointed look again. But whatever. He wasn't a play type of guy.

"Dude! What was that all about?" Tyler asked when he finally sat down with his lunch. "Did she bust you for the note thing?"

Sam shook his head, his mouth too full of sandwich to speak. Finally he swallowed. "Nah, it was nothing to do with that. She was just asking . . ." He wanted to tell Tyler and laugh about it—to make fun of the idea that he would ever do a school play. But somehow he couldn't bring himself to say it out loud.

"It was nothing," he said. And, at the urging of the others at his table, he started telling the story of the drowned girl.

Chapter Thirteen

IN WHICH THERE IS A PRE-THANKSGIVING DISASTER AND NEW TRADITIONS ARE BORN

TO: LUCY_CUPCAKE
FROM: PAPABEAR
SUBJECT: RE: TG PLANS

Hey, Luce—

Are you ready to come north and work your magic? I should warn you, we're all particularly spicy this year. Frog hasn't stopped talking about your coming since Halloween was over. (Unless, that is, he's talking about his imaginary best friend, Ladybug, who he swears is real, despite the fact that she wasn't at the school open house or his friend's birthday party because of a mysterious rash. Don't ask.) Also, if you get a chance, talk to E-man. He's clammed up pretty good about his new school. . . . Tom says to let him be, but I figure he might just talk to you. You're his favorite aunt. Of course, you're also his only aunt.

And you make cupcakes for a living. Anyway, we'll pick you up at the train Tuesday. Brace yourself.

Love,

Bro

P.S. Frog brought the pickled shark-in-a-jar you got him from that store in SoHo to school. His teacher apparently almost fainted and asked Frog to put it in his bag. He did, but only after waving it around the circle. His classmate Noah promptly threw up (which, in fairness, he does with alarming frequency). So thanks for that.

Frog loooooved visiting Lucy in New York. He loved the yellow taxis that would stop if he put his hand up and yelled loudly enough. He loved that fire trucks were always driving by, at any given moment of the day or night. He loved the American Museum of Natural History, where he could lie down under the dinosaur bones or stare at the biggest diamonds he could have ever imagined. He loved the Central Park Zoo, where he had a very special friendship with a red panda. But what he loved most of all was his aunt Lucy.

Lucy was the best. She didn't have a car, and didn't even know how to drive, but she would take all four of them on the subway, and could ride it carrying a bicycle or anything else. She told Frog she once brought a tent, a pair of snowshoes, and a cooler downtown during rush hour and never even got yelled at. She kept a leash in her closet for Flare, because she said New York was far too busy for a cheetah to walk around without a leash. She cooked the best food in the world, and told them she learned everything she knew from studying take-out menus left on her stoop. Also, she was rich, all from her baking. And not just any baking. She made cupcakes so famous that people wrote about them in magazines and had her mail them around the world. Getting rich on cupcakes . . . Frog couldn't imagine anything better. And best of all, when they were with her, she told them that, unless it endangered their health or well-being, the answer to any question they asked would be yes.

"Can we get sugar cereal?"

"Yes."

"Can we go to the zoo every day?"

"Yes."

"Can we have ice cream from the place down the street for breakfast?"

"Yes."

Visiting Lucy was the best thing ever. This year Lucy was coming to their house for Thanksgiving, and while it wasn't quite as good as going to New York, it was still awesome. When she got to their house, Lucy cooked practically the whole meal, and made around a hundred different pies, and always let them help with whipped cream and stuff, even when it got all over the kitchen. He couldn't wait.

"The best part of Thanksgiving is that it's really like a Christmas and Chanukah preview," said Jax, curled up by the fire as the rain poured down. It was barely an hour after school, and it was already almost dark out. They were hanging around, waiting until it was time to pick up Lucy. Frog was bouncing on the couch, too excited to sit. Next to him, Zeus moved in time with Frog's bounces.

"Is it almost Chanukah?" Frog asked, bouncing. "Last year we lighted the candles at Lucy's house!"

"No, it's late this year," Jax said. "Not till practically Christmas."

Frog looked disappointed.

"But still, all the Christmas lights are up, and there are wreaths and stuff outside the supermarket," Jax continued. "It smells so good. *And,*" he said, "I can't wait for the street hockey game with Hen and those guys." On the years when the Fletchers spent Thanksgiving in Shipton, Henry's family, the Garcias, joined them.

"The best part of Thanksgiving is that Lucy will bring rugelach," said Sam with a dreamy voice, clearly thinking about the crisp, fruit-filled pastry.

"Stuffing," said Eli. "Definitely the best part of Lucy's

Thanksgiving is the stuffing. She puts sausage! In the stuffing!"

Frog couldn't help bouncing even more. Zeus gave him a disgusted look and jumped off the couch.

"The best thing about Thanksgiving is LUCY!" Frog shouted.

Frog was about to tell everyone (again) why he loved Lucy, but before he could start, Papa's office door opened and he came out, his phone pressed against his ear. Without saying anything, he held his hand up to the boys, telling them to wait.

"So how bad is it?" Papa asked. His face was worried.

Frog assumed he was still on his work call, and started again, in a whisper this time, to tell his brothers why Lucy's visit was going to be great. Papa was silent so long that Frog began to forget he was there. So it was a surprise when Papa swore, a big, loud four-letter word that would require a hefty fine.

"Jason, did you say something?" Dad called from his office upstairs. "Is it time to go?"

"Oh, he said something all right!" Sam answered gleefully. Lately Sam had been paying quite a lot in fines. "He said—"

"I don't need a direct quote!" Dad said. He was now standing in the stairwell. "Jason . . ." He didn't continue, as Papa began to speak again.

"Ohhhh, my poor Booger!"

Jax snickered. Papa's nickname for his younger sister was Booger—*not,* Lucy was quick to point out, because of what was in her nose. She had named their first cat that, and Papa had never let her forget it.

"How bad a break is it?" Papa asked.

At this they all went silent.

Papa nodded, though of course Lucy couldn't see it.

"Uh-huh, yeah. Well, I guess that's lucky. How long do the doctors think you'll need the cast? . . . Six weeks! . . . Yeah, okay."

He was silent again. Then he laughed. "Are you nuts? If you're not supposed to exert yourself, then coming here is the last thing you should do!"

The room erupted in noise, each Fletcher shouting questions and not waiting for answers.

Finally Frog shouted, "I'm going to throw up all over Eli unless someone tells me what's wrong with Lucy RIGHT NOW!"

Once again, the room fell silent. Frog had been able to vomit on command since he was three and had refused to try fish. No one doubted his word.

Papa waved a hand at all of them and hissed, "QUIET. NOW. OR ELSE." He looked really mad. "Are you sure?" he said into the phone. "It sounds like a terrible idea to me." He listened for another moment, then groaned. "Fine! Be that way. I'll come down tomorrow morning, and we'll drive up early Thursday."

He was silent again. "Don't be silly. You're not taking the train. They'll do just fine getting dinner ready. If you insist on coming, then you're riding with me. Period."

Slit-eyed, the boys stared at one another. Frog felt like throwing up for real, or crying. What was going on? What did Papa mean they could get dinner ready themselves? He glowered at the coffee table and forced himself not to cry, barf, or—worst of all—talk.

Finally Papa hung up the phone. "Here's the deal," he said before anyone else could speak. "Lucy broke her arm trying to navigate up the stairs of the building with some enormous table her neighbor needed help moving. She called from the hospital emergency room. Her friend Rebecca is with her, and the doctor said it was a pretty clean break. But she'll also need to spend the night at Rebecca's because she hit her head, and the doctors don't want her to be alone.

"Now. I think she should stay put and rest, but apparently she's too crazy to do that. So I'll go down and pick her up tomorrow, and we'll come back as early as we can on Thursday. We'll see how it goes. But all of you are going to need to help Dad. The shopping's all done, and I'll do what I can tonight on food prep, but Dad and the rest of you have school tomorrow, so you'll have to work hard to pull off a Lucy-style Thanksgiving."

Immediately the boys all started talking.

"We can help! We can start right now. Do you want me

to make chocolate chip cookies?" Sam asked. It was the only thing he knew how to make.

Dad shook his head. "I don't think we need cookies, but thanks," he said. "Now let's see. Henry's parents will bring salad, and no doubt Lucy has desserts in her freezer she'll want to bring up. But we can maybe peel the squash tonight, and at least wash and trim the green beans. . . ." He kept talking as he wandered into the kitchen with Papa.

Frog was deeply relieved. It was still happening. Lucy was coming. "We'll all help! Totally we will! How hard can it be?"

He was about to find out.

"Sam, find the cumin. CUMIN. *C- U-* . . . Oh, forget it. I'll find it myself."

Dad was rattled, and Frog really, really, *really* didn't want to get in his way. It was Thanksgiving Day, and Papa was on his way back from New York with Lucy. The plan had been for Boppa and Mimi, Papa's parents, to come early to help with the cooking. They lived only two hours away. But they had gotten stuck in traffic behind a seven-car pileup.

Jax skulked along the edge of the kitchen, probably hoping to not get in the way either. Some stuff had gotten done before Papa had left. And they had tried to get a lot done yesterday, but somehow he and his brothers had ended up having a massive mud fight in the yard. Jax had said it was to celebrate, and that settlers had probably been a lot dirtier because they didn't have bathrooms and stuff. Dad had said that by the time they all had showers and baths it would be a take-out pizza and straight to bed.

Now, at twelve-fifteen, the Fletchers-minus-Papa were supposed to be making the squash. Well, squash, green beans, mashed potatoes, stuffing, and cheddar cheese buns, but . . . for now, squash.

Jax, peering through the spices, defended Sam. "It's not Sam's fault. . . . None of these are labeled! What does koobin look like anyway?"

" 'Cumin,' rhymes with 'human.' Not 'koobin.' And it's a kind of brownish-orange color," said Dad, not looking up from the recipe. "We also need chopped thyme, cream, pearl onions— Drat! We were supposed to have already blanched, cooled, and peeled them! Quick, Sam, put a pot of water on the stove on high!"

By Frog's estimation it was turning into a lousy Thanksgiving. Dad was amazing at lots of things. He helped coach Frog's and Sam's soccer teams and taught them how to ski, and he also made tacos and really good chocolate-butterscotch-chip cookies. But unlike Papa, he didn't really cook anything else. And even though he had sworn to Papa that they would be fine, the preparations didn't look, to Frog, at least, like they were fine at all.

"Here," Jax said finally, throwing a small plastic bag full of orange powder at Dad. "Here's your koomin, or whatever."

"Thanks," said Dad, throwing a few big spoonfuls into the saucepan. "What time is it? Has that water boiled yet? Frog, why don't you help Eli set the dining room table. Remind him to use the fancy silver and the big tablecloth. Jax, start peeling potatoes while Sam and I try to finish up this squash." He turned to see if the water was boiling yet, only to find that Sam had lit the wrong burner and the water was still cold. He let out a noise between a shout and a groan.

Frog was about to ask Jax if he was planning to do anything nice for Mr. Nelson for Thanksgiving, since the Halloween party hadn't done the trick. For the past few weeks Jax had been talking about the research he was doing at school. It sounded cool, though the real-life Mr. Nelson was no friendlier than usual—he'd been in his yard looking mean during the mud fight the day before. But as Frog was going to ask, there was a hissing splashing from the stove as something boiled over.

Frog scrammed. He found Eli hard at work, but not on setting the dining room table, which was still covered with books and homework and Frog's own pinecone-and-acorn centerpiece.

"What are you doing?" Frog asked, peering over Eli's shoulder. "Ooh, neat! Can I try?"

Eli was carefully breaking tiny twigs and gluing them onto pieces of birch bark. Each one spelled a name.

"Sure. You can do Dad. Just do the *D*s like this." He showed Frog how to use three straight sticks to make the *D*.

Frog got right to it. And other than Eli's having to remind him to use vowels, he was pretty good.

It was fun work, Frog thought. Kind of like letter tracing at school. He hummed happily to himself, lost in the twigs. Then the smoke alarm went off.

"What's that?" Eli shouted, dropping the Mimi twigs onto the floor and knocking over the glue. The noise was so loud that Frog felt like he could see the vibrations.

"Fire! There's a fire! We need to stop, drop, and roll! We need to open the window!" Frog yelled, dropping everything.

"Wait! Don't freak out! Dad and Sam are cooking! Let's just . . . Ahhhh," Eli said.

The noise had stopped. In the silence Frog exhaled slowly, not realizing he'd been holding his breath. He hated loud noises. He didn't even like fireworks. "That was . . . YIIIIKES!" The alarm started up again. It seemed louder than before.

Over the alarm, they could hear Dad screaming, "Open the window! Just open it! I don't care if it's raining in!"

"Dad!" Eli shouted. "Daddy! Should we go outside? Where are Sir Puggleton and Zeus?"

"No! Everything's fine!" Dad swore, loud and fierce, and suddenly the noise stopped again.

"What's going on?" Frog was nearly in tears.

Dad's face appeared in the kitchen doorway. Frog was relieved to see there was no smoke, no flames, and no burns anywhere.

"The squash just bubbled over and burned onto the bottom of the oven," Dad said.

"That's it?" Eli asked incredulously. "A little burned squash?"

"That's all. Now, is the dining room all set? I need you to start the cranberry stuff. It's nearly two o'clock."

Uh-oh. Frog glanced at Eli, whose wide eyes suggested he too had forgotten the dining room.

"Um . . . we're just getting the extra chairs. It'll be done in a minute," Eli said.

They waited for Dad to explode, but he just ran his hands through his hair, making it stand up even worse than usual, and then dashed back into the kitchen, where they could hear him yelling at Sam to leave the window open and never mind the wet floor.

Frog didn't think it was a good time to tell him that he'd stepped in the glue.

Chapter Fourteen

IN WHICH JAX TRIES TO PLAY THE GAME

> Dear Mr. Nelson,
>   We thought you might enjoy some Thanksgiving dinner. Sorry there's no turkey. But the crispy beef is really good.
>   —Jax Fletcher

By the time three o'clock came, every single one of the cooking Fletchers had either cried or threatened to quit, but the two kinds of cranberry, the squash, the cheddar buns, and the green beans were all ready. The dining room was clean, since Frog and Eli had shoved absolutely everything that had been in there—from Papa's laptop to

Sir Puggleton's roll of poop bags—into Papa's office, and they had finished the place cards. Sam had retired upstairs and fallen asleep as soon as he'd been relieved from duty. Dad was lying down with a pillow over his face. Frog was asleep curled up on his chest.

Eli had sprawled by the fire to read. Jax was tempted to bug him to play a game or something. He knew he should think about more diplomacy efforts toward Mr. Nelson, but he was just too exhausted. There was still loads of time. According to the timeline, he was supposed to start the interview in January or February. And yeah, it was probably a good idea to get Mr. Nelson to agree to do it, but Jax still had a few months to butter him up. The report wasn't due until spring, after all. And he was so tired! Cooking, it turned out, was brutal. Before he knew it, he was asleep right in the chair.

When he next woke up, it was to an almost dark house and the sound of Papa's and Lucy's voices in the hall.

"Anyone here? Helloooo?" Lucy called.

Jax sat up and scrubbed at his eyes.

"We're all asleep! We're here!" Frog yelled, and jumped up just as Dad groaned and rolled into a sitting position on the couch.

"Are they here? Is it three? Wonderful," he muttered, rubbing his eyes and reaching for his glasses.

It had to be later than three, Jax realized. The sky outside was nearing sunset. Blearily he followed Frog into the hall, where Papa, Lucy, and a bunch of promising-looking shopping bags were waiting.

It took a while for everyone to wake up and kiss Lucy and sign her cast, but finally it was done. Frog had taken the longest, drawing a yellow taxi, a cupcake, and, just because it was his favorite thing to draw, a pine tree.

Papa came over and gave everyone a kiss. "How did the cooking go? Any disasters?"

Dad shook his head, stretching and groaning a little.

"It went. There were a few mishaps, but we managed. What time is it? Have you heard from your folks?"

Papa nodded. "They're off the highway—finally—and will be here any minute," he said. "That traffic was unbelievable. And the Garcias should be here soon too. It's almost four o'clock," he added, wandering toward the kitchen and talking over his shoulder.

There was a moment of silence, and then he spoke again from the kitchen.

"Um . . . Tom?"

"Yeah?" Dad answered, still on the couch.

"Do you mind coming in for a second?"

"Uh-oh, you're in trouble!" Jax and Eli sang out to Dad as he walked into the kitchen.

The kids could hear their fathers' voices. "It's totally fine, but . . ." Papa paused. "Did you make the turkey?"

There was a silence.

Lucy and the rest of the Fletchers walked toward the kitchen. Jax's mind was racing. Had they made a turkey? They'd made everything else, even the two different kinds of cranberry sauces! But the turkey? He suddenly remembered the giant white-wrapped thing that had been in the way all day as they'd tried to get different ingredients out of the refrigerator.

Lucy rushed in. "Tom, it's fine! It's not a problem! Don't panic! We can just—"

At this moment the doorbell rang.

"Everyone's here!" Frog announced.

In the kitchen, everyone started talking at once. Dad was apologizing; Papa was questioning; Eli, Sam, and Jax were explaining; and Lucy was trying to assure everyone that the turkey would barely be missed.

Papa picked up the phone. "I'm calling Shanghai Gardens," he said loudly, cutting over everyone else. "The heck with it. We have squash, biscuits, and all the fixings. We'll add a little Peking duck and crispy beef."

"And don't forget spareribs and dumplings!" Eli shouted.

That night, fourteen of them sat around the beautifully decorated table, complete with Frog's pinecone-and-acorn centerpiece, twig place cards, and two different kinds of cranberry sauce. Unfortunately, the squash, which Papa tasted before he brought it to the table, had been seasoned with hot pepper powder, not cumin, causing Papa to spit it into the sink and madly rinse out his mouth with milk. That was excellent, and Jax begged to be allowed to serve some to Henry, who had been in the dining room when it had happened. But even without squash, the meal looked delicious.

Dad proposed a toast. "To Jason and Lucy, who always make this look easy, and to the boys, who certainly now know it's not. This is the best one yet!"

Jax, moving the stuffing over to make room for the Chinese spareribs and fried dumplings, had to agree.

The traditional post-meal street hockey game was taking longer than usual to get off the ground, and Jax was getting annoyed. First Sam ate so much that he had to lie on the floor with Sir Puggleton for half an hour, groaning and holding his stomach. When he finally got up, it was to see if there was any leftover pie! It took forever to get him out the door. And now here was Henry, messing around with the phone he had gotten the week before for his tenth birthday. Fletchers didn't get phones until they were twelve, and Jax hated looking at it.

"Are you coming?" Jax said finally. He knocked his hockey stick onto the floor, just in case Henry forgot what they were supposed to be doing. Sam, Eli, Frog, and all the Garcias were already outside making teams.

"Yeah, I'm just sending one last text," Henry answered, not looking up.

"To who?" Jax asked. It was Thanksgiving. Who was even looking at texts?

Henry snapped his phone shut and shoved it into the pocket of his jeans. Jax noted with disgust that they were his fancy jeans, dark and tight-fitting. Apparently Henry was looking at him too.

"What are you wearing?" he asked. Jax had thrown on an old pair of sweatpants. He'd learned the hard way that street hockey almost always meant a ripped knee.

Jax looked down at himself. Admittedly, the sweatpants were a kind of bright red, and a little too small. But who cared? It was street hockey. "What? Not fancy enough for you? Want me to have some swag jeans like yours?" He had meant it to sound funny, but it had just come out sounding mean.

Henry shrugged. "I just texted Miles and a couple other guys that we're playing on your street if they want to come out. That's all."

Jax looked down at his too-small red pants one more time. Dad yelled from outside.

"Hey! Boys, are you coming?"

Jax made a face at Henry. "Whatever. Let's just play." He started toward the door, Henry behind him. But his grandmother Mimi called to him before he got outside. She and Boppa were cleaning up, shooing everyone else out of the kitchen to play hockey.

"I made up the plate of food for your neighbor. Can you bring it over to him?"

Jax groaned. He had told Mimi and Boppa all about the Veteran Project and how he wanted to make Mr. Nelson a little less—what was the word Dad had used? Hostile. That was it. Dad had talked about diplomacy, and the need to warm up relations between factions before asking Mr. Nelson for anything. Anyway, so far the thunderstorm at Halloween and the flowers Frog had thoughtfully collected to help him out hadn't done much good. It had been Mimi's idea to bring him some food.

"Sure, Mimi, I'll take it," he said. "But I'm not sure it will work. He's still pretty much a jerk to all of us. I probably should have chosen a different veteran." Jax paused for a second.

"Hey, Boppa, you're around the same age as Mr. Nelson. Did you fight in a war?"

Boppa shook his head. "No, I was in college when soldiers were fighting in Vietnam. And college kids didn't have to fight. It made a pretty good argument for staying in school."

"Yeah, I was just researching it. So there was a draft, but not everyone got drafted, right?" Jax asked.

"That's right," Boppa said. "It was a rigged system. It

was mostly—not always, but mostly—the poor and less educated who fought that war. And it's not that there's no honor in serving your country. There is. Your great-grandpa was in the service. But when it came to Vietnam, pretty much nobody wanted to go if they could help it. And kids like me, with families to help pay for college, well, we got off easy. Your Mr. Nelson might have signed up himself, but most boys who went over there didn't have a choice. You might want to ask him about that when you interview him."

Jax nodded. It was a weird thought, that maybe Mr. Nelson had *had* to fight and his Boppa hadn't. But he didn't have time to think about it now. Grabbing the plate, which was covered in foil and smelled delicious, he headed out.

"Be right there!" he called to the teams, and he walked over to Mr. Nelson's. The porch light was off, and Mr. Nelson's Buick was in the driveway. Jax was nervous as he rang the doorbell. He practiced under his breath.

"This is for you. Happy Thanksgiving," he whispered to himself. But no one came. After putting the food down, he scrounged in his pocket for something to write a note on. He had a pencil stub and a napkin, which was wrinkled but clean. Leaning against the wall of the house, he wrote quickly.

"Hey, Fungus-Brain! Get over here!" Sam yelled from the street.

Jax hissed in frustration. First Henry and now this! He placed the note carefully on the plate, turned, and ran to join the game.

The game, once they finally agreed on teams and Dad swore not to check anyone and Frog came back from building Flare a nest of blankets on the porch and Henry looked at his phone a few hundred more times, was awesome. Dad and Henry's parents—Matias and Amelia—had all played hockey, so they were a little scary to play against. But Sam was almost as tall as Amelia now, which wasn't saying much—Jax figured she had to be the shortest hockey player in the world—and Matias had messed up his knee and refused to run, so the teams were evenly matched. Henry's little sisters were pretty fast, and both were in the beginner hockey clinic, so they were actually kind of good teammates. They all kept playing even though it was completely dark, even though Jax was bleeding from both scraped knees (and yes, the pants had ripped), even though Sam said he was starving and needed to go in soon to eat. The only reason the game ended, finally, was that Miles and Ronan and Jessica and Madison showed up, and Henry stopped in the middle of everything to talk to them.

No one else seemed to mind calling it quits; Sam actually ran inside to get a plate of leftovers. But Jax wanted to keep playing. Henry had barely played, taking endless time-outs to check his phone, and putting it away only when his mom threatened to take it. And now here he was, still clean and not even sweaty, joking around with Madison and goofing with Miles.

"So, do you guys want to come in?" Jax said. He felt like he didn't really belong here, which was stupid, because it was his house.

"I might just go change," he added when no one answered. "Be right back."

He dashed upstairs, shucking the ripped and dirty sweatpants off as he ran. His Thanksgiving pants, which were nothing special but at least had no visible stains, lay on the floor where he had left them. Jax looked at them for a second before diving into his closet for his newest jeans. They weren't tight like Henry's, but at least they were pretty dark.

Running back downstairs, he heard Papa call to him.

"Do the boys want to come in for round two of food?" he asked. "Who's out there anyway?"

"It's just Ronan and Miles. And some girls," Jax added. "I think they just want to stay outside."

Papa exchanged glances with Matias, who was playing checkers with Frog. "Okay, bud," Papa said. "But not too long. It's a family holiday, after all."

Jax nodded and ran out. Miles and Ronan were wrestling on the lawn, and Henry was talking up some scary

TV show. Jax had never heard of it. It didn't seem like any of them had even noticed he'd been gone. Finally, after around fifteen minutes of this, Madison shivered.

"Jess, we need to go home. You ready?"

Jessica, who was blabbing about some other TV show Jax had never heard of, nodded.

"We'll walk you back. You guys want to walk with us?" Miles asked.

Henry nodded. "Let me just text my mom," he said, pulling out his phone.

"She's right inside! Just tell her!" Jax exploded. "And besides, it's dark." He knew he couldn't walk the girls home, even though they lived around the corner. Papa had already yelled out a five-minute warning.

Henry looked up from his phone. "It's just down the block. My mom says it's cool. You coming, J?"

"Nah. I'll catch you guys later," Jax said. He hoped he sounded casual, like he just wanted to hang out at home instead of going with them. It was seven-thirty, and completely dark.

"See you," Madison said, and Jessica echoed her.

Jax nodded and wrapped his arms around himself as they walked away. Standing there, he noticed a shadowy movement on Mr. Nelson's porch. The food! He had forgotten all about it. Maybe this would be his chance to say something nice, maybe even mention the project. . . .

Moving closer to the edge of the yard, he squinted,

trying to see what was there. Just then Mr. Nelson's porch light blazed on and the front door swung open. Jax barely had time to register the black-and-white creature that was snuffling around the plate of food. The next thing he knew, Petunia, Mr. Nelson's yappy little dog, darted out the door, her leash attached to someone still inside. Jax tried to shout, but it was too late.

"WHAT THE— PETUNIA, NO!" Mr. Nelson's voice was loud and fierce, but it didn't stop Petunia from running toward the skunk. Seconds later the smell shot through the air. Jax knew it was cowardly, but he didn't care. He dashed inside as fast as he could, breathing hard and praying Mr. Nelson hadn't seen him. Once again, he had failed at diplomacy.

Chapter Fifteen

IN WHICH ELI STRUGGLES

Eli, it was so good to see you. Thanks for making it such a special Thanksgiving. . . . I didn't even miss the turkey. Did you? And sorry about your neighbor's dog and the skunk. Bummer. Anyway, I can tell that you are perfectly happy, if by happy you mean looking mad and sad and grumpy every time I mentioned school. Call anytime, okay, amigo?

Love you, Lucy

The Monday after Thanksgiving it rained. At Pinnacle, rain meant there was no outdoor recreation time. But instead of having free time in the cafeteria like at his old school, here they went to the gym for mental and physical gymnastics. This, Eli had learned, meant push-ups mixed with times tables, and jumping jacks blended with spelling. He hated it.

"Receive: *R-E-C* . . ." There was a long pause while Griffin struggled with the *i*-before-*e*-except-after-*c* rule.

119

Eli's foot was cramping from all the jumping he was doing, and his bangs were sweaty and stuck to his forehead. His arms dropped to his side and he stood panting, the smell of sweat and gym and damp stuck in his nostrils.

"Fletcher! What about you?" Mr. Bleau bellowed. "Think you can spell 'receive'?"

"R-E-C-E-I-V-E," Eli answered, his voice monotone. "Can I go to the bathroom?"

"May I," Mr. Bleau corrected. "By fourth grade I think we can assume you can." He chuckled at his joke, then turned back to Griffin.

Eli skulked off to the bathroom before Griffin could butcher another word. He moved soundlessly in the empty hallways; the building was built with some fancy environmentally repurposed flooring that muffled sounds, even when a hundred kids all moved at once. His lonely footsteps didn't even register.

When he got into the bathroom, he slumped against the wall. It was feeling like the worst day ever, and he didn't even know why. His mind wandered back to the conversation he'd had with Lucy.

"Soooo . . . tell me! I haven't heard a word about Pinnacle School! How has it been?" Lucy asked. "It's been more than two months already. That's enough to get a good taste, at least."

They were walking to cut down a Christmas tree. With her bright red-and-purple knitted cap, her red wool coat, and the cast, Lucy looked like an accident-prone elf.

Eli didn't want to answer. "It's fine, I guess."

He hoped she'd let it drop. The whole point of Thanksgiving was to have a break from thinking about school. But Lucy wouldn't drop it. She just stared at Eli.

"What?" he asked. "I'm fine!"

"I'm not saying you're not fine," Lucy said calmly, still staring at him. "I'm just saying, call anytime. And also, don't be so smart that you act stupid."

"What's that even supposed to mean?" Eli asked.

"It means, don't sit and stew over whatever's bugging you. Talk to me, talk to your dad and Papa, talk to Sam, but thinking you've got no one to talk to . . . that's stupid."

In the bathroom now, Eli put his face in his hands and rubbed, hard. The last thing he wanted was for anyone to think he'd been crying in here. Stupid or not, Eli wasn't about to tell anyone—at school or at home—that Pinnacle wasn't what he'd hoped. He had chosen it. He had begged. So what if there were no games. Or free time. So what if his stomach hurt every lunch period because they had to eat in silence so as not to waste time. It had been his choice. Papa always said you had to live with the consequences of your actions, and Eli knew he just had to live with the consequences.

The door opened suddenly, and Mika walked in. He looked at Eli.

"What are you still doing in here? Bathroom breaks are five minutes, maximum. You've been in here at least seven," he said.

Eli blinked hard and looked at his watch. He knew exactly how long he had been in here. Six minutes and thirty-eight seconds when Mika had barged in. Eli realized early on that the longest bathroom break he could get away with was seven minutes forty seconds, and he used every bit of it.

"I'm coming," he answered Mika.

Mika answered from inside a stall. "You'd better be. Because you know the rules. 'If anyone's tardy, the whole class pays the price.' And I'm not missing snack because of you."

He came out banging the stall door. While Mika washed his hands, Eli made his escape.

"Well, I'll see you back in there," he said. Mika just nodded.

Back in the hallway, Eli checked the clock that hung outside the gym before he went back in. Fifteen more minutes. Fifteen more minutes of spelling and jumping. It didn't sound that bad. But then Eli thought of the months rolling out ahead of him, and his eyes prickled again. The consequences were going to roll on forever, and he would have to live with it.

When Dad picked him up that day, Eli couldn't be bothered to make small talk. Usually he tried to make the days sound . . . if not great, then at least pretty good, though Dad didn't seem to buy it. Most of the time, Eli would assure Dad that he was just thinking, and that was why he wasn't talking much, and Dad would finally leave him alone. Today he was just too tired. Mr. Bleau had yelled at him when he'd come back to the gym; by Eli's watch he had been gone for eight minutes fifty seconds, which was way beyond what he could get away with. So he'd had to do extra laps. It wasn't that he minded running. The running actually felt good. It was just that everyone else watched him being punished and didn't say a word. At least he hadn't made them miss snack.

"You okay, E-man? You're even quieter than usual these days," Dad said. He was looking into the rearview mirror, trying to catch Eli's eye. "School's still good, isn't it? Your teacher sure thought you were doing excellent work when we met her at the parent-teacher conference. Are you worried about swim lessons starting up again?"

Eli just shrugged. Swim lessons were no big deal. Neither was piano, or walking Sir Puggleton, or helping sort laundry, or anything. In fact, Eli figured that in terms of different things in his life, he was lucky that the largest percentage of things were good. But the small percentage of things that were bad took up the greatest percentage of his time. He was busy trying to figure out how he would write down this equation, when Dad spoke again.

"Are you getting along okay with the kids at school? It seems like most of the time you want to get together with Jamil or Teddy or one of the other Shipton guys, but we can try to get more playdates going with Pinnacle kids."

"No. Really, it's fine," Eli said quickly. The last thing he wanted was his dads to see how Griffin, Mika, Ethan, and most of the other boys in the class treated him. Ambrose was nice, at least, but he lived pretty far away.

"Okay, but let me know. Those kids are going to be your classmates for a long time, and it's a while before you'll have a driver's license," Dad said. He glanced back again, maybe hoping to see Eli laughing at his joke.

Eli tried to smile. But the thought of being at Pinnacle, while the rest of his brothers rode their bikes and played with their friends, and yes, goofed around at recess, made his heart hurt. He squeezed his fist until his fingernails bit into his palm. He had begged to go to Pinnacle. He had no one to blame but himself.

Chapter Sixteen

IN WHICH THE PLAY TRYOUTS ARE DISCUSSED–AGAIN

Unknown Number:
Hey—it's me, Em. So psyched you're doing it!
CU 2morrow. GL!!!!

Sam couldn't stop whistling the tune from *Wicked*, the musical Lucy had taken him to in Boston after Thanksgiving. It had been so awesome—he couldn't believe it was the same old story of the Wizard of Oz that he had seen a million times. And the music! He had to stop himself from humming it in school. The play was just so cool. There was no other word. It was kind of weird and dangerous and . . . cool. He had tried to tell Jax about it, but Jax had been baffled.

"The girl singing is the green-faced mean witch?" Jax had asked.

"Yeah, but . . ." Sam had tried to explain that she

wasn't really mean, and that her sister, the so-called good witch, was really a pain, but Jax's eyes had drifted away.

"If you say so," he'd said doubtfully, and he'd changed the subject to the indoor soccer league that was starting that week.

Sam knew better than to bring it up with Tyler or any of the other guys at school. But when he glanced at the seat next to his in homeroom, he saw that Emily Shawble's binder was covered with stickers, including—he had never noticed!—a *Wicked* sticker from the play. When he looked closer, he saw it was surrounded by stickers from other plays. Some he had even seen: *Oklahoma!, Annie, Peter Pan*. His dads were big fans of musicals; they even played the sound tracks on long car rides.

He was curious. Clearing his throat, he pointed to the *Wicked* sticker. "Have you seen it?" He immediately felt like an idiot. Obviously she had, or she wouldn't have a big sticker of it.

But Emily shook her head. "I've never seen it, like, professionally done. But I was in it at the community rep theater last year." She smiled. "What about you?"

Sam felt a little less dumb. "Yeah, I saw it in Boston last week. It was awesome! What part did you play?"

She looked slightly embarrassed. "Elphaba. You know, the green one."

"The lead." Sam was impressed.

"Yeah, well, it's only youth theater, but . . . Boston! That must have been amazing!"

Her enthusiasm was catching, and before long he was telling her about the elaborate sets, the special effects, and the way the floor disappeared whenever the scene changed. Before long they were the only two talking in the classroom, and Ms. Daly and all the other kids were staring at them.

Sam's face burned a dark, serious red. "Sorry," he mumbled. He looked down so he wouldn't see Keith and Tyler smirking at him from across the room. Keith was kind of a meathead, a hockey player who hung out with him and Tyler because he lived across the street from Tyler, but he looked far too ready to tease Sam over talking about plays. Sam never really felt safe around Keith. He was funny, but you never knew when you were going to be his next target.

As soon as homeroom was over, Sam moved quickly out of his seat, not wanting to give Emily another chance to start talking. When Emily walked by, he talked loudly to Tyler, making it a point not to catch her eye.

But Emily seemed determined. She tracked him down the next day, and in spite of himself Sam was kind of glad. *Wicked* had been unbelievably cool, and Emily was curious about all the different things the Boston show had done. From there they talked about a few other plays Sam had seen, almost all of which Emily had acted in at some point or another. Then she asked about the play tryouts.

"I heard you telling ghost stories in the cafeteria after Halloween," Emily said as they were walking in from recess.

Sam grinned. "Yeah? Which one?"

"The one about the girl whose doll came to life and tried to stab her. Totally freaked me out! My sister collects those fancy china dolls with the painted faces that look creepy anyway, and after that . . ." She shuddered. "I make her close her bedroom door. I don't want their little glass eyes staring at me!"

Sam laughed.

"Anyway, you're really good. What part are you hoping for?" Emily continued.

Sam tripped over a backpack left on the floor and dropped his lunchbox. Grapes flew everywhere.

"Huh? I'm not an actor. I've never even been in a play! I play soccer!"

Emily bent down to help him gather the skittering grapes. "So do I. Central midfield. What does that have to do with anything?"

"Well, it means I don't have time to be in some play! The tryouts for the Elite Team are in the spring, and I'm going to need to practice, like, every single day this winter. And besides . . ." Sam was about to say he wouldn't want to anyway, but somehow he couldn't quite say it. "I don't know anything about it."

Emily stood up and dumped her handful of grapes, as well as an eraser nub and a crumpled-up math sheet, into the trash. "It's not that much to figure out. You tell stories—kind of like you did for Halloween. But instead of having to do all the voices, other people do some of them. And besides, you can still play plenty of soccer. I think a bunch of coaches are renting gym space every Monday and Thursday for pickup games. You'd get plenty of playing time there. That's what I'm doing, anyway. You should at least check the play out. You'd be great as Rooster. Can you sing? I think you do okay in chorus, but I can't remember."

"Rooster?" Sam asked. "Sing? Um, yeah, I can carry a tune. But . . ." He trailed off, dumping his own dusty grapes and going to his seat. He hadn't even looked closely enough at the posters to see what play it was. Emily followed him.

"Rooster Hannigan, Miss Hannigan's criminal brother," Emily said. "You know, *Annie*. Have you ever seen it?"

Sam nodded. They had seen it last summer in Maine. It was pretty good, with fun songs.

"I'd rather be Oliver Warbucks," he said, without even thinking.

Emily's eyes lit up as she went back to her own seat. "Even better! He has some great songs. So you'll do it? See you after school tomorrow."

Sam rubbed his eyes. Somehow he had just agreed to try out for the school play.

Chapter Seventeen

IN WHICH JAX IS SURPRISED

Jax—

Please STOP setting up the Havahart trap
at the far edge of the yard. You have now
caught Mr. Nelson's dog TWICE when the
poor thing was having a pee at the edge of the
bushes. Once was embarrassing. Twice is just
ridiculous. The skunk will just have to live without
being relocated. I know you were trying to ease
hostilities by helping Mr. Nelson out and getting
rid of it, but given the circumstances, I believe
giving up is the better part of valor.

Love, Papa

P.S. You are going to have to ask him about
this project soon. Your teacher talked about it
on parent-teacher conference night and seemed

It was the lamest winter ever. Rain. Almost every day. Jax knew that officially winter didn't start until December twenty-first, but in Shipton, after Thanksgiving it was supposed to snow.

As he trudged home from school in the warmish, dull rain, Jax was bummed. There were no outdoor football games in the yard, no driving to the beach to see if the seals were out, and certainly no snowball fights or sledding.

"Jax! Wait up! Hey, Jax!"

Henry was running toward him, his raincoat unzipped and flapping behind him. The rain plastered his hair across his face.

"Hey!" Jax said. Finally maybe something fun would happen. "What's up, man? You want to come over for a while?"

Henry had been busy practically all the time since Thanksgiving. First there were indoor lacrosse practices, because suddenly Henry had decided that he wanted to play lacrosse in the spring instead of soccer. Then there were the times he was over at his neighbor Ian's "hanging out." Whatever their hanging out was, it never seemed to include Jax.

"Dude! I was just going into the gym to grab something, and I heard your brother. In there. SINGING!" Henry was breathing so hard, he could barely speak. He bent over and braced his hands on his knees, catching his breath.

"What? What are you even talking about? Which brother?" Jax was confused.

"Sam! What other brother would be in the gym at school? He was singing some kind of rap song about a cat. It was funny. But . . . he was singing!"

Jax wasn't sure what to say to this piece of news. It was weird, sure, but maybe Tyler and a bunch of guys were goofing—

"You know what's going on today, don't you?" Henry pressed. He had apparently caught his breath and was standing up, sticking his wet face right up under Jax's hood. Jax could smell Henry's Trident Tropical Twist gum and whatever he'd had for lunch earlier.

"Um . . . no. And get out of my face! Did you have tacos for lunch? Ugh."

Henry was unfazed by the insult. "No, burritos. But, dude, today is the school play tryouts. You know, when all the artsy lalalala types try to get the lead so they can run around in makeup. What's he doing?"

The rain started to pick up. It was warm and damp, and Jax could see rain or sweat on Henry's forehead. It was stupid weather for December. He started walking again, lowering his head against the wet.

"I have no idea. If you're that interested in what he's doing, you should have stayed and spied longer."

Henry started walking too. "I wasn't spying. I was getting my hoodie, and I just heard him. Belting it out. Like some actor dude!" He was silent for a minute, walking alongside Jax. Jax wished they could talk about anything else. He tried desperately to think of something to say, something funny that would make things go back to normal with Hen. But Henry spoke again before he'd thought of anything.

"Do you think he was doing it as a joke? Like maybe Tyler or Keith were going to go next, just for fun?"

"Whoa, are you taking my name in vain? What's up, nuggets? Where's Sam-bone?"

Jax hadn't even heard him, but suddenly Tyler was beside them, jumping off his skateboard and snapping it up into his hand.

"I thought Sammy was with you, Fletcher junior," Tyler continued. "He told us he had some family thing after school."

Jax looked up. Sam had lied to Tyler? This wasn't good.

"Uhhhh . . . uh . . . ," Jax stammered, unsure what to say. But Henry butted in.

"Dude! Don't you know? He's trying out for the school play. Like, now." Henry's voice rose excitedly, and he coughed, trying, Jax was sure, to sound cool for Tyler. "I heard him. Seriously, it was kind of wack. He was singing."

"Singing?" Tyler sounded disbelieving.

"Well, doing a funny cat rap song."

Tyler smiled. "Yeah, that's pretty awesome, actually. But what the hey, man? The play?" He shook his head, his wet hair splashing Jax in the face.

"Tell your bro to text me when he gets in. Stat. Okay, nugget?" he said.

Jax just nodded.

Tyler skated off, spraying water behind him. Henry and Jax kept walking, Henry yammering the whole time. "I wonder if there's some girl in the play. Or maybe he's doing it as a joke. Without Tyler or those guys." His voice was doubtful.

Jax wanted to defend his brother, but his brain was too muddled. Sam, in the school play? Sure, the family liked going to musicals and stuff. And Sam had loved that one he'd seen with Lucy. But the school play? It was kind of weird. Still, why did Henry care so much anyway? He'd talked more to Jax today about the dumb play than he had in weeks. Jax tried to think of something else they could talk about.

"So have you started your Veteran Project interview?" he asked after a few minutes of silence.

Henry nodded. "I'm almost done. It was so lame. I just emailed a bunch of questions to my cousin Neil and he answered them. What about you?"

Jax groaned. "Haven't even really started. Stupid Mr. Nelson. I've been trying to, you know, get him less mad at us, but it hasn't really worked."

Henry laughed. "Dude, why do you even care? Just find someone else. Heck, I can ask my cousin if you want another name."

Jax didn't answer for a minute. The truth was, he really wanted a chance to talk to Mr. Nelson. He'd searched Google for Mr. Nelson's name after Thanksgiving, and had found out he was actually a pretty cool guy. There had been an article in some paper about how he'd been part of the last group of soldiers in Vietnam, and been on a ship that had gone back to rescue a bunch of families trying to escape. But Jax wasn't sure he could tell the new, cool Henry all of this. He just shrugged.

"I've already started a ton of research," he said. "I think I'd better just stick with him."

Finally, after what felt like an ice age of walking, Jax turned into his yard. "So, do you want to come over and hang out?" he asked. He didn't really expect Henry to say yes, and sure enough, H. was walking away already.

"Not today, man. I've got lacrosse later and Ian's mom is driving us. Sorry," he said.

"Sure. Well, see you," Jax said. He went inside, shutting the door tightly behind him. He'd hoped Henry would make this lame day better, but now it had only gotten worse. For a minute he thought again about the article he'd read, and wondered if he should just go over and knock on Mr. Nelson's door. But the rain beat down on the windows, and Jax sighed. Maybe tomorrow he'd do it. Today was already bad enough.

Chapter Eighteen

IN WHICH IT IS THE YEAR OF THE PUCK, AND ELI APPLIES THE PRINCIPLES OF ARCHIMEDES

TO WHOEVER FINISHED THE COOKIES
AND PUT BACK THE EMPTY BOX:
We are collecting clues and are hot on your trail.
Be warned.

"Holy Mackinaw, has it gotten cold!" Papa came in from walking Sir Puggleton, rubbing his hands together and stomping his feet. Sir Puggleton, for his part, gave a huge doggy sigh, as though the walk had exhausted him. Papa had picked Eli up today, as Dad had a late meeting, but Eli hadn't gone with him on the walk. Too much homework.

"Well, the unseasonable warmth is gone, and winter is nigh. You all know what that means, right?" Papa asked.

Eli was the only one in the room, not including Sir Puggleton and Zeus. And he was trying to get through his mountain of work. But Papa didn't wait for an answer.

"It means it's rink time! Are you ready? I think this is going to be the year of the puck. Officially. I'm planning a dedication ceremony. Who's with me?"

Eli finally looked up. "Papa, I'm the only one here. Jax slammed straight up to our room, Frog walked next door to Katie's house, and Sam isn't home yet. He called while you were walking Sir Puggleton and said he was staying at school to work on something. And I'm trying to get my homework done! I have fifteen math sheets. Plus a report comparing and contrasting a lima bean and a black turtle bean. In cursive!"

The cursive was the breaking point. Eli hated cursive. His homework load was so bad that the Fletcher Family Rule about nobody having free time until all homework was done had been dissolved back in October.

Papa's smile didn't waver. "Bah! I spit on your lima beans! I will write you a note saying you were excused for an exercise in experiential learning entailing the freezing point of water and the rate of volume fill per cubic foot."

He went over to the closet and started pulling out warm gloves, boots, and hats.

"Jax!" he hollered in the direction of the stairs. "Get your butt down here! It's Operation Great White North!"

Jax grumbled something through his closed door. Eli turned back to the math sheets.

"Gentlemen! If you want a rink, get moving. NOW!" Papa's voice was muffled as he bent over to pull on his boots.

Eli looked up, sighing. "It's not even cold out."

In answer, Papa threw open the porch door, which was next to the table where Eli was working. A blast of frigid air swept his papers onto the floor.

"JAX!" Papa bellowed again before Eli could respond. "NOW!"

Eli bent down to gather up his work. "But . . . it was so warm earlier."

"A cold front is coming through. It's supposed to be cold for the next five days. . . . If we move, we could be skating by the weekend!"

Eli couldn't help being a little excited. The winter before, they had built an ice rink in the yard, laying down plastic and filling it with water. Eli wasn't much of a hockey player—he had no real desire to be smashed up against the boards—but he loved the rink and the hot chocolate and campfires that went with it. Leaving his papers in a messy pile, he started to pull on his still-damp rain boots and look for his gloves.

Jax appeared at the top of the stairs. His face was surly. "What do you want?" he called down to Papa.

"YOU, my little ray of sunshine! I want you to get yourself down here and help us. It's rink time!"

Like a mask falling off, Jax's sulky expression vanished, and excitement took over.

"Seriously? Really? But it was pouring—it's totally warm and gross out!"

Papa started out the door. Turning, he said, "Don't trust the weather in New England. Cold front's coming. It's the year of the puck!" With that he slammed the door behind him.

Jax sprang into action. "Hurry up!" he said, even though Eli was already dressed and he was the one standing in a pair of pajama bottoms and no shirt. "We have to help! Let's go!"

"I'm ready," Eli said, annoyed. "And where's Sam, anyway? We're going to need him to help move the boards."

Jax's face grew grim again. "Don't ask. I'll be right down." He slammed back into their room to get dressed.

With a sigh, Eli pulled on his gloves. The rink was so much fun, but . . . all that homework! It was just going to be waiting for him. And Papa might say what he wanted about spitting on his lima bean, but the fact was, he had to do it before tomorrow. And in cursive.

"Cursed cursive!" he said out loud.

"Huh?" Jax asked. He was back, dressed to go outside.

"I have to write a compare-and-contrast report on beans. In cursive!" Eli's voice was glum.

"Oh." Jax seemed disinterested. "Bummer. But I guess that's the Pinnacle way. Anyway, let's go!"

Sam didn't get home until almost dark. Eli and Jax had been struggling to carry the boards between them, and Frog, who had returned from Katie's, only added to the work, offering to help but really just getting in the way.

"Finally!" Eli said, sweat steaming up his glasses. "Where have you been? Papa's all spazzed out about getting the rink up tonight. I guess it's going to be cold for a while."

"Gee, really?" Sam asked sarcastically, shivering in the T-shirt and raincoat he was wearing. "I hadn't noticed." But he was smiling. "I'll be right out to help."

When he came back out bundled up, Jax rushed over to him. Eli didn't know what they were talking about, but he figured it was some Upper El thing that didn't include him. He sighed.

With Sam's help the rest of the boards were in the plastic brackets in no time. By the time Dad drove in, home from his meeting, the five Fletchers were lined up, ready to unroll the giant plastic liner that would go under the water.

"Remember," Papa said, "this is a critical step. If it rips, if one of you pulls too tightly, the whole thing will—"

"Poop the bed!" Frog shouted. This had become one of his favorite expressions. "You know, get all messed up!"

Papa sighed. "Yes, it will get messed up. But, Froggie, please don't say—"

"You say it!" Frog interrupted.

"ANYWAY," Papa said firmly, moving on. "It's a critical stage. So everyone walk forward sloooooowly, unrolling at the same time."

Dad honked the horn and waved out the open window. "What can I do?" he asked, stopping the car.

"Get the hose," Papa called. "We're ready to roll!"

As they headed back into the house, Eli's nose was running and his fingers were tingling. His brain was tingling too. Dad had asked him to calculate how quickly the rink would fill if it was seventy feet long, forty feet wide, they needed ten inches of water, and it was filling at a rate of eight gallons per minute. Eli was desperate to get his hands on a pencil and some paper to try to figure it out. But before he could even get started, there was a shout from the doorway.

"Daddy! Papa! The rink is broken! Water's pouring out!" Frog yelled.

Papa said a word they were not allowed to repeat.

"What happened?" asked Dad, pulling his shoes back on.

"One side collapsed. Look!" Frog pointed. Sure enough, the heaviest boards, on the side where the yard sloped slightly, had fallen over, and water was pouring out.

Everyone ran outside. Sam put his shoulder to the board and tried to push it back into position, but it wouldn't budge.

"All together!" Papa yelled, his feet already soaked with icy water as he climbed through it to try to grab the board from the other side. But even with them all pushing and pulling, they couldn't get it back into position.

"It's no use," Dad said, standing up from where he had been trying to hold the board in place. "We'll have to stop the water, fix it, then refill."

Papa groaned.

Eli looked at the board. Surely there was a way. He knew water was stronger than people realized. Still . . .

"What about a lever?" he said suddenly.

"What?" Papa asked.

"A lever. If we got . . . I don't know, a big stick under it, and braced it on something, maybe we could kind of pry it back into place."

Dad looked excited. "Leverage! Good idea, E-man! Sam, go grab one of the pieces of lumber from behind the shed!"

Papa gave Eli a big, terribly cold, and wet hug. "A lever! 'A lever,' says my brilliant son! You know who used a lever? Who was it who said, 'Give me a lever and a place to stand, and I can move the world'?"

Eli didn't have time to hear the answer. Sam was back with the wood, and in the freezing cold, the Fletchers moved as one to push the board back into place. As soon as it was back in the plastic bracket, Dad grabbed the piece of wood and fashioned a brace behind the board, reinforcing it.

There were high fives all around.

"Archimedes!" Papa yelled, hugging Eli again. "That's who! Tonight we drink a toast to Archimedes and the principle of leverage. Well done, Eli!"

As everyone went back in, after one more reassuring glance at the now sound rink filling up again, Eli felt good in a way he hadn't in weeks. Give me a lever and place to stand, and I can save the rink, he thought. For the moment, he didn't even care about lima beans.

The next day, however, was another story. As expected, Eli got reprimanded for not finishing his compare-and-contrast essay and had to stay in during morning recreation to complete it. Now it was afternoon, time for project work.

Eli knew he was smart, and therefore he knew that he understood the number one hundred and ten. And he was also smart enough to know about relativity—that a number feels different depending on the circumstances. One hundred and ten chocolate chip cookies, for instance, would look like a ton. One hundred and ten grains of sand, on the other hand, would seem like a tiny amount. And one hundred and ten bee stings would be horrible, while that many jelly beans wouldn't even seem like that much. Unfortunately, the Pinnacle School was falling closer to the bee sting side of the list than the jelly beans. And while there were one hundred and ten days left of this year, next year would be almost two hundred more. And still more the year after that. Eli didn't know how he could bear it. Each day was another sting—of teachers who told you only what you could do better, of other students who were suspicious if you wanted to see their work.

Mika was the worst. "What are you looking at?" he asked Eli, who had wandered over to his table. He put his arm protectively over his project.

"I was just curious. I'm doing a bridge model too. But mine's a drawbridge—it won't bear as much weight as yours, but I wanted to build a pulley system. I was just curious how yours was coming," Eli said.

"Well, DON'T BE." Mika was clear. "Do your own work. Jeez."

Sting. "I'm not copying, Mika! I already finished mine. I just thought—"

"Well, don't think, then. Leave me alone." Mika scowled and turned toward the teacher. "Ms. Gallwin! Eli is distracting me!"

Eli took a step back. Distracting each other was the worst thing students could do at Pinnacle; it was *not* the Pinnacle way. Griffin had been sent to the principal's office for repeatedly distracting the class by talking about the football play-offs. Turned out his cousin actually played for the New England Patriots and was willing to come into the school, but it would have been too distracting.

Sure enough, Ms. Gallwin came over, her face ominous.

"Eli Fletcher. Surely there's something productive you can do other than distracting Mika, hmm? Have you finished already?"

Eli nodded.

"Well, that doesn't mean you are free to wander around creating a distraction and tempting others to procrastinate, does it?"

Eli tried to explain. "I was just curious, since we're both working on bridges. I thought—"

"Uh-hummm. Well, let's just find something more productive to do, don't you think?" Ms. Gallwin said.

Eli hated that everything she said ended in a question. He felt his cheeks get warm.

"Actually, no, I don't think." His voice was a little too loud for the "quiet working volume" they were required to keep. But he didn't care.

"I actually think it would have been productive to share

147

ideas. I just read a book about engineers, and believe me, they did a lot of brainstorming together! They didn't think that talking to another engineer was distracting! I would have considered it productive to share ideas with Mika, if he weren't such a jerk!"

There was a moment of silence in the class before an excited buzzing broke out. It sounded, Eli thought, as he went to gather his bag for his trip the principal's office, a lot like a swarm of bees. One hundred and ten days. How was he going to bear it?

Chapter Nineteen

IN WHICH FROG MAKES COOKIES, BUT *NOT* WITH LADYBUG

TO: LUCY_CUPCAKE
FROM: PAPABEAR
SUBJECT: Oh, you'll love this
Hey, Luce—

As promised, here's the Christmas/Chanukah/ Kwanzaa/etc. list from the boys:

Sam: Minecraft (version 12.3.5.6, I believe), iTunes gift certificate, new hockey stick (but be warned . . . it has to be a "sick" one), and for books, "something as awesome as Harry Potter"—good luck with that.

Jax: The newest Wimpy Kid book, a new football (don't ask what happened to the one you gave him last year, I have no idea), "the same hockey stick as Sam's"

Eli: Lego architecture kit—either the Guggen- heim Museum or the Lincoln Memorial (these cost a fortune, just so you know). Feel free to come up with a substitute.

Frog: Well, he wants a kitten and peace for all the animals, but I forbid the former, and I don't really know how to approach the latter. Maybe a science kit and a stuffed animal instead?

As for me, well, can you possibly give me a way to get through a whole workday without finding someone's underwear, lunch, or mitten on my computer? That'd be great. Thanks.

Love, Bro

"Twelve days, twelve days, twelve days of Chanukah, fa-la-la-la-laaaaa!" Frog sang as he waited for the school bus with Papa.

"Last I heard there were eight days, Froggie," Papa said.

Frog danced up and down a little. "It's a song me and Ladybug made up. We added more days, like the twelve days of Christmas." He paused. "Even though Christmas only has one day."

"Ladybug and I," Papa said automatically. Then he frowned. "Your class isn't doing religious stuff, is it?"

Frog nodded enthusiastically. "We're doing them all! All the religions! All of them."

Papa looked skeptical. "'All of them' meaning a million Christmas-tree-and-stocking crafts and one lousy clay menorah, or what?"

"No, I mean all of them. We went around the class and told what religions our families are, and then we made a picture of them all. Ahmed is Muslim; Noah, Rob, and Lily are Jewish, like me; Ladybug and Han are Buddhist and Christian; and Grace, Harry, the other Noah, and everyone else is Catholic. Or Christian, which is some other kind of Catholic, I think. Also like me! Plus I'm Hindu. So we're doing them all." Frog was breathless from his recitation.

Papa looked impressed. "That's a pretty good mix. So what are you doing to celebrate everyone?"

"Well, I told you Ms. Diane wants you to come in on Thursday and make latkes, right?" Frog was still bounding around, kicking at the frozen slush on the side of the road. "A couple kids in my class asked what latkes were, and I told them they were kind of like those potato things we got at the McDonald's drive-through once with Mimi and Boppa, only way better."

The bus was pulling up, and there was a sudden rush as all the other kids moved to get themselves into some kind of a line. The windows of the bus were steamed up, and it was impossible to see inside.

"Wait! NO! You certainly didn't tell me I'm supposed to come in and make latkes for twenty—"

"I think there are forty-three of us. It's both Ms.

Diane's and Ms. Kim's classes. I got to go! Ladybug's saving me a seat!" Frog shoved his way into the line. "Love you, Papa! Bye!"

When Frog got home with Papa at the end of the day, he was greeted by the smell of gingerbread. "Ohhhhh, is it time? Is it?" he asked as they walked into the house. "Why didn't you wait for me?"

"Sam just started them a little while ago," Papa assured him. "He wanted you to be able to decorate some right away."

"Yay! That's the best. It's even better than the best, because I told Ladybug to ask her moms if she can come over today, and if she does, we can decorate them together." He looked at the clock. "The little hand is near the four, so does that mean it's almost four?"

Sam had been looking at Papa over Frog's head, rolling his eyes about something. But Frog didn't care.

"Close, buddy," Papa said. "It's around ten minutes after four. . . . See how the short hand is after the four? That means . . ."

His voice trailed off when Frog left the room. "Hey! Where are you going?"

"To find Ladybug's phone number! She gave it to me so you can call her mom! Also, their cat is going to have kittens soon. Can we have one?"

Frog walked back in, slightly disappointed. "Hmm, it got a little ruined. But I think I remember it." In his hand was a damp scrap of paper, the numbers barely legible.

"Can you try calling, Papa?" he asked.

Papa took the wet paper and squinted at it. "Froggie, I can't even read this. Is that a nine? Or a four?"

"Let me see," Frog said, grabbing the paper back. "A four. I'm almost sure."

Papa shook his head, but went ahead to the phone anyway.

Frog stood watching, wiggling excitedly from side to side. "Is she answering?" he asked in a loud whisper.

There was a loud buzzing sound from the phone that Frog could hear all the way from where he was standing. Papa hung up.

"There's nobody at that number," Papa said, and he sounded a little annoyed. "Why don't you just make cookies with your brothers. After all, tonight's the first night of Chanukah. You won't have that much time to decorate them."

Frog was disappointed, but the promise of cookies now and latkes and presents later soothed him. Before long Jax and Eli wandered into the kitchen, and Sam was kept busy pulling cookie sheets out of the oven. Frog's cookies were largely decorated with red blobs of frosting.

"It looks like he's been shot with a machine gun," said

Jax critically, looking at a particularly splattered ginger-bread man.

"It's fine," Frog said, unconcerned. "I'll start using blue. Then it won't look like blood."

Eli was busy painstakingly drawing pin-striped pants on his gingerbread man. Sam just squirted frosting on them and shoved them directly into his mouth.

"What time is it now?" Frog asked after a while. The house was warm and smelled delicious. If only Ladybug were there! Outside it was almost dark. Getting close to the shortest day, Dad had said at dinner the night before. The day with the least sunshine before the earth turned and the days started to get longer.

"It's late. This is the last batch," Sam said, banging the oven door shut. "And you guys are on cleanup. My work here is done."

"Any news about you-know-what?" Jax asked around a mouthful of cookie.

Frog looked up from his decorating. "What's you-know-what?"

"Nothing!" Sam said quickly. "Jax, I told you to shut it. It probably won't matter anyway. So mind your own business unless you were hoping for a new face." He scowled and left the kitchen. Frog quickly went back to his cookies. He'd learned to leave Jax and Sam alone when they argued, or they'd both wind up mad at him instead.

Jax made a rude gesture behind Sam's retreating back,

then turned to Eli. "Rock, Paper, Scissors to see who cleans up?" he asked.

Frog finished his last cookie. They looked so good! He wished Ladybug could see them.

"Maybe that number was a nine. Do you think Papa would try to call her mom again?" he asked.

Jax and Eli ignored him.

"Guys? GUYS! Can I ask Papa to call Ladybug's mom, or is he on a work call?" Frog said louder. Sometimes his brothers acted like he wasn't even in the room.

Jax lost, his paper getting cut by Eli's scissors. "Give it a rest!" he barked at Frog, slamming the trays into the sink. "Go play with your imaginary friend upstairs. Leave us out of it!"

Frog's mouth dropped open. He looked around to Eli for support, but Eli had fled. "What? You're mean! And you're not even right. At all! Ladybug isn't imaginary. She goes to my school. Stupid!" His voice quavered a little on the last word. They weren't allowed to call each other stupid. Would Jax tell Papa? Or worse, Dad?

But Jax didn't look like he was going to call Papa. Instead he just turned on the water and banged the sheets against the sink.

"If she's real, find me her name in the school phone book. Go on! I'll wait." He made a big show of turning off the water and standing against the sink, his arms folded and his foot tapping.

"Fine!" Frog stomped across the kitchen and found the Grove Elementary directory. He turned the pages with vigor, too mad to remember what letters came after what. After paging violently from one end to the next, he looked up at his brother.

"Her last name starts with *L*. Is that before or after *F*?"

Jax crossed the kitchen. "Give me that!" he said, grabbing it from Frog's hands. Frog bit back a yelp of frustration. He just wanted help. He could do it. But he kept quiet.

"Here." Jax thrust the book under his nose, so close that Frog had to cross his eyes slightly to see it. "Here's the *L* page. Do you see anyone with the last name 'Li'? Anyone?" Jax shook the page.

"Stop it!" Frog screamed, and grabbed it back. He scanned the page. He couldn't read well, it was true, but 'Li' was easy, just two letters. It wasn't anywhere on the page.

Rage bubbled up, and in misery he felt the beginning of tears forming in his eyes. He blinked them back. "That book is WRONG! It's stupid! It's . . ." He hesitated for a second, but only a second. "It's a MORON!" he shouted at the top of his lungs.

There was a moment of silence, during which Jax scampered back to the sink and started washing cookie sheets as though his life depended on it. Moments later, Papa's voice was heard coming closer down the hall.

"Excuse me? EXCUSE ME? What exactly is going on here?"

Frog fled to his room, sobbing. This was turning out to be the worst cookie day in history.

Later, after Dad came down from grading papers and Eli emerged from his homework and the rest of the boys gathered, Papa brought the old brass menorah out of the dining room cupboard. Frog was still miserable; Papa had been angry at him for yelling, and worse, had refused to try the phone number again with a nine instead of a four. Still, there was a cozy fire in the family room, and the pile of presents on the couch made him feel a little bit better.

"Now," Papa said, "before we light the candles and say the prayers, I just want to make sure everyone is okay. Eli, no trouble at school today?"

Eli shook his head. He had told the family over dinner the other night about his visit to the principal's office, and Frog had been both surprised and a little impressed that his hardest-working brother was suddenly breaking rules.

"Jax, you're still doing research at school for your Veteran Project?" Papa continued.

Jax nodded, looking pained. "Yeah. But I guess I'm supposed to fill in a basic information sheet before winter break. You know, my veteran's full name, dates of service, rank, and all that. I can get it from Google, but it's supposed to be through a verbal or written interview."

"Well, I guess it's time to knock on Mr. Nelson's door, then," Dad said. "After all, the diplomacy efforts don't seem to be doing much good. Maybe you should just jump in."

Jax shrugged. "Yeah. I guess. Maybe."

Papa nodded and turned to Sam. "And how about you? Any news?"

"Nope." Sam answered so quickly that Papa had barely finished his question. "Everything totally normal. Nothing to report."

Papa and Dad both looked at Sam for a few seconds, but Frog had had enough. The presents were gleaming in their corner. The menorah candles—only two this first night, the *shamash,* or helper candle, and one other—were in position. And the ingredients for the potato latkes were just waiting to be fried up in oil.

"Can we light the candles now? PLEASE?" Frog yelped. Everyone jumped a little.

"Sure, Froggie. Let's get to it," Papa said. "Sam, as the oldest son, do you want to do the honors?"

Sam took the matchbox from Papa, struck the match, and lit the *shamash.* He began the prayer, and the rest of them joined in.

"Baruch ata Adonai, Elohainu melech h'aolam . . ."

The prayer went on in Hebrew, which Frog didn't

understand but had memorized, then in English. Then they sang, and told the story of the miracle of Chanukah, of the Jews whose small amount of oil had lasted for eight days and eight nights while they'd worked to make more. Then, finally, it was time for presents and latkes.

"Thank you, Dad! Thank you, Papa!" the boys all shouted as they tore off the bright tissue paper to find new woodworking kits, animal books, hockey gloves, and T-shirts.

"Thank you, boys," Dad said as he showed Papa the modeling-clay-and-candy-cane menorah Frog had made them.

They were all talking at once, and Frog was happy again. He forgot his fight with Jax, and how mad he had been. It was Chanukah, and there were seven more nights to go. Maybe tomorrow he could play with Ladybug.

Chapter Twenty

A FLETCHER CHRISTMAS

Dear Santa,

My brother Sam is writing this for me, and he says it can be from him too. Mostly I just wanted to say thank you for always coming every single year and bringing presents. I really, really, really, really want a monkey this year, but I know that might be hard. Sam said he didn't know if you could bring live animals, and I said I know you can because my friend Gabe at preschool got a dog from you once. You might remember him. His dog is really big and bit his sister. Anyway, if a monkey is too hard, then I guess I just mostly want everyone in my family to be happy and live a really long time and die when they're really old of old age. And I want the Playmobil pirate ship too, I guess.

Merry Christmas, Santa.

Love and hugs and kisses,

Frog (my real name is Jeremiah

Fletcher, but I think you know that)

P.S. We are leaving you potato latkes instead of cookies. Eli says you get lots of cookies and might not ever have tasted a latke. They're really good.

Jax wanted to ask Eli if anyone had ever actually died of excitement. Like, if their heart couldn't take the pressure and exploded. He lay back on his bed and stared up at the ceiling. Eli was on the lower bunk beneath him. If your heart exploded, did it actually explode outside your chest—actually burst through? The thought was totally sick. But it was more likely that it just—

"*Stop* it!" Eli said from below.

Jax's whole body lifted a foot off the bed. "Jeez! Why'd you want to scare me to death? Are you trying to see if my heart bursts outside my body?"

"Huh? I just want you to stop kicking," Eli said, his voice muffled. Eli liked to sleep like a mummy, wrapped under numerous layers of blankets.

"I wasn't kicking," Jax protested, before he realized he had been swishing his legs back and forth under the blankets and knocking against the edge of the bunk. "Oh." He stopped. "Sorry."

Eli grunted in response.

Jax was silent for a minute, but he couldn't contain himself. Even though he knew Eli loved to sleep, Jax had to talk or he would explode. He sat up and peered over the side of the bed, though there wasn't much to see in the darkness.

"Is Frog asleep?"

"Yes. It's the middle of the night. Probably even Sam's asleep by now," Eli grumbled.

"But it's Christmas Eve! Tomorrow is Christmas! Have you been awake all along? Have you heard anything? I thought I heard something."

There was a scuffling as Eli sat up, and after a minute his voice sounded much more alert. "You did?" Eli asked. "What did you hear?"

"I'm not sure. It sounded like some kind of thumping on the roof. But really fast."

"It could have been squirrels," Eli said doubtfully. He was clearly awake now, Jax was relieved to hear. It was always better to have a brother or two awake. Until last year all four Fletcher boys had slept in one room for Christmas Eve, with Sam and Frog sleeping on the floor in the room with Eli and Jax. But Sam finally rebelled, saying that he was sure Santa was going to purposely save their house for last because they were the last people awake in the whole time zone. Now he slept in his own room.

Jax and Eli were both silent for a moment. On the floor, Frog shifted slightly.

"I don't hear anything," Eli said finally. And Jax had to agree. He lay back down.

There was more scuffling as Eli burrowed under his blankets again. "Wake me if you hear something," he said from within his cocoon.

"I will," Jax said, staring up at the ceiling again. "I'm going to stay awake all night. I'm definitely going to hear him this year. I'm not even a little bit tired. Actually, I think I might—"

"Quiet!" hissed Eli.

"Sorry," whispered Jax. "But I'm just staying awake. I'll . . ." He yawned hugely. "I'll keep you posted. . . ."

The room fell silent.

"Wake up! Get up, you lazybones! Don't you want to see if Santa came?" Sam's voice barged through the silent room, where all three younger Fletchers had been sound asleep.

"Wha— What time is it? Darn it!" Jax sat bolt upright in bed. "I fell asleep! I missed it!" He looked at the brightness outside the blinds. "What time is it?"

"Almost seven o'clock! It's the latest you've ever slept on Christmas. Let's go!"

Eli was already up and pushing past Frog to get out the door. Frog, still groggy, was trying to get out of the sleeping bag that had somehow gotten twisted around and around him.

Jax leaped off the top bunk and landed close to Frog, who yelped and rolled out of the way. "Watch out!" he squeaked. "You nearly landed on Shaman!"

"Who the heck is Shaman?" Jax asked.

"Flare's baby brother. He's visiting for Christmas," Frog answered.

Jax ignored this. "Christmas! Christmas! Merry Christmas!" he yelled, running down the stairs. He repeated it as though he were sounding an alarm.

Before long, a fire crackled; stockings exploded in colorful wrappings all over the room, (including a small one for Zeus and a slightly larger one for Sir Puggleton); and Dad and Papa looked slightly more awake, clutching cups of coffee.

"Seven-ten. That's a new record," Papa said, sinking into a chair.

Jax grimaced. "I wanted to stay awake all night and hear the sleigh. Or maybe the train—you know, like in *The Polar Express*. But I fell asleep."

"It's just as well. The closer you peer at a mystery, the further it recedes," Papa said.

"I like that. Who said that?" Dad asked curiously.

Papa laughed. "I don't know. Me, I guess. I just made it up!"

Jax made a face at him, then shoved more chocolate drops into his mouth.

"Can we open the big presents now? Can we?" Frog asked.

Jax looked over. "Frog! You haven't even seen what's in your stocking! Did you even look at what you un-wrapped?"

Sure enough, Frog was sitting in a pile of torn wrap-ping paper, his fingers itching to unwrap still more, but at Jax's words he looked over as if surprised at the pile of presents next to him.

"Oh! Cool! Santa brought those new markers and the Spider-Man I wanted!" he said.

"Yeah, and check out those cars! Sick!" said Jax, shuf-fling over on his knees to check out Frog's haul. Trust Frog not to even know what he had! Jax had already memo-rized every whoopee cushion, race car, comic book, and baseball card from his stocking. It was time to check out the rest of the stash.

The morning passed in a blur of paper, boxes, double-A batteries, and the excitement of knowing that more people—and more presents—were arriving later in the day. Dad and Papa were impressed with their homemade potato-battery-powered light, which Eli and Jax had built, and seemed delighted with Sam's and Frog's choices of books for them—*The History of Cod* for Dad, who seemed to think it wasn't actually the most boring book in the world, and a book about the New England Patriots for Papa that Sam started reading as soon as it was un-wrapped.

Then it was time for skating on the rink, followed by hot chocolate and a chance to review presents and be de-lighted all over again with new books and comics. As the day darkened, Jax sat in a chocolate-and-skating-fueled haze in front of the fire. Maybe just a little nap before the dinner guests arrived . . .

Staring into the flames, with Sir Puggleton leaning co-zily up against him, Jax dozed.

It wasn't until that night after dinner that Jax remem-bered the thought he'd had while waiting for Santa.

"Hey, guys," he said, sitting up and moving Zeus off his lap. "I have to drop off the card and other stuff we made for Mr. Nelson—remember?"

The boys had made a number of holiday items for Mr. Nelson, from Frog's cotton-ball-beard Santa to a pretty cool-looking star ornament that Eli had made out of twigs. They had also made some gingerbread cookies that were safely closed in a tin. Jax had even taped the tin shut for good measure; he didn't want another skunk. His plan had been to drop it off before vacation—and to fill out his information sheet while he was at it. But then Ms. Sugarman had extended the deadline. Jax, relieved, had decided it could be a vacation project.

Papa snored a little from his spot on the couch. He had been dozing since dinner, occasionally rousing himself to play a game of chess with Eli before dropping back off again.

But Dad looked up. "That's a nice idea, Jax. I'll walk over with you. I saw the pile of stuff you printed out. . . . Mr. Nelson's pretty interesting, don't you think?"

Jax nodded. Vacation was almost two weeks long. He'd definitely get to the interview sometime. Maybe Mr. Nelson would even come over to thank them for the gifts, and they could all sit down together.

The air was cold and crisp, and burned like ice in his throat when he inhaled. He looked up into the night sky. It was perfectly clear, with a fingernail moon rising over the trees beyond the yard. Jax, his arms full of presents for Mr. Nelson, felt suddenly and unaccountably happy. The food, the presents, the little bit of snow that had fallen just in time for Christmas Eve . . . it was all wonderful. He gave a shiver of delight. He hoped Mr. Nelson would like his card, and that the diplomacy would finally work. With all the magic of Christmas, he knew it just had to.

Chapter Twenty-One

IN WHICH NEWS IS SHARED

TO: LUCY_CUPCAKE
FROM: PAPABEAR
SUBJECT: FOR SALE: BOYS
Dear Luce—

Do you think I could find a buyer for four used-but-still-serviceable boys? Although I'd have to be honest and say they're not really working properly. Honestly, Lucy, why don't these guys come with instruction manuals (or at least warranties)? They are either wing-nut crazy, which is worrying, or absolutely miserable, which is of equal concern. I think I'll move to Australia.

Love from your bro

Once Christmas was over, the whole house felt like a balloon with the air leaked out of it, or at least, that was how it seemed to Sam. Most of their friends were away or had family visiting, and even the new stuff from the holidays was boring after a week of constant use. To make matters worse, a thaw had turned their rink to slush. Papa assured them the weather would get cold again soon, but for now, the rink was just a big puddle.

Jax was mooning around, complaining of being bored; Frog was grumpy because, he said, Ladybug was away visiting grandparents and wouldn't be able to invite him over for a playdate; and Eli . . . well, who knew what was going on with Eli. He was spending most of his time in his room, building bridge models and refusing to explain his bad mood. Both Papa and Dad took him out separately for Special Guy Time, Fletcher code for one-on-one time with a parent, but when they came back in, Eli looked just as miserable, and his parents looked defeated. Finally they just left him alone.

Now it was the last day before school started back up. Sam himself was on edge. He was waiting to hear if he got into the play, and it was with equal parts dread and excitement that he checked his phone for the text from Em that the list was posted.

With nothing else to do, he wandered up to Eli and Jax's room. As expected, Eli was crouched on the floor surrounded by tiny pieces of balsa wood, and Jax was on the top bunk listening to music. Sam paused in the doorway.

"Either of you guys want to play knee hockey in the hall?" he asked.

Eli didn't glance up. "Not really," he said.

Jax looked up questioningly and removed a headphone. Sam repeated the question.

"Maybe. Not right now," Jax said.

Sam sighed. He wandered over and idly picked over the piles of stuff on Jax's desk. "Oh, cool, you did that crystal growing project," he said, looking over a report with a red check plus in the top corner. "Looks like you nailed it. You're probably going to start the mousetrap cars after break."

Eli looked up at this. "You make mousetrap cars?"

Jax had put his headphones back on, so Sam answered. "Yeah. Fourth-grade science has some cool experiments. After the mousetrap cars I think we did models of the earth's structure."

Eli looked surprised. Then, like a curtain falling, his sullen look came back. "Whatever," he said. "It's not like it has anything to do with me."

"What's your problem?" Sam asked. "You've been a pain all week. What's even wrong with you, anyway?"

"My problems are *my* problems, and they're none of your business," Eli said, glaring.

Sam turned on his heel and left. Sometimes his brothers were incredibly lame.

Sam went back to the family room, where Dad was

reading by the fire. Finally Jax trudged in, his face grouchy. "Can we watch cartoons?"

Dad looked up from his book. "No, you guys already had plenty of screen time. I thought you were going to play knee hockey. That sounds fun."

Jax snorted.

"Or if you're looking for something to do, maybe we should walk over to Mr. Nelson's and see if we can't get him to take a little time for the interview. He never got back to you after we dropped off those gifts, did he?" Dad asked.

Jax shook his head. "Not even a note. Anyway, I don't have to do it until after vacation. We got an extension. And I don't really feel like it right now. And actually, I don't want to play knee hockey either."

"Well, why don't you call Henry? I saw Amelia at the store last week, and she said they're around."

Jax just shrugged and sighed, then trudged back out of the room.

Dad sighed too and called after his retreating back, "Okay! I give up. Stay bored and grumpy if you want." He turned to look at Sam, who was refreshing his phone's messages. "And what's with you and that phone?"

Sam blinked nervously. He hadn't bothered to tell his parents about the play tryouts—auditions, as Em called them. He figured there was plenty of time to bother with that if he got in.

Just as he was trying to think of an excuse, a message popped up with a pinging noise. But not from Em, from a strange number. Sam held his breath as he skimmed the words.

> Hi, Sam. This is Ms. Daly. I hope it's okay to text you—your contact info was on the audition sign-in sheet. You were the unanimous choice for the part of Oliver Warbucks! Hopefully that's good news! But I wanted to touch base before posting the cast list, because if you don't want the part, or don't think you can make the commitment, we will make another choice. Let me know, and feel free to call if you want to talk.

Sam's heart sped up, and he realized with a jolt that he was excited, really excited to get that part. The funny lines, the rich-guy costumes, even the songs were kind of fun and cool.

"Good news?" Dad's voice was a surprise, and Sam jumped.

"Huh?"

"You just said 'YESSS' and did a kind of fist pump thing. So . . . good news?" Dad said again, gesturing to the phone.

Sam felt like his smile was going to take over his face. He needed to text Em! But first he needed to let Ms.

Daly know he wanted it. Or did he? When he'd talked to Tyler after the tryouts, Tyler had been kind of okay about the whole thing, but what would Josh or Keith or even Coach Javi say? Even Jax thought it was weird. "Um . . . yeah. Good news. I um . . . I just got into the school play."

Sam hadn't realized that Papa had come into the room or that Jax had wandered back in from the kitchen, Frog on his heels. They all stared for a second, then began to babble all at once.

"What? Wait—back up."

"What play? When were auditions? Why didn't you say anything?"

"Did you get the lead? Will you wear makeup?"

The questions came so thick and fast that Sam couldn't even tell who was asking what. He held up his hands.

"Hang on! Quiet already, and I'll tell you!"

"Be QUIET!" Frog said loudly, even though everyone had stopped talking.

Sam took a deep breath. "Emily Shawble talked me into auditioning for the school play because she said my stories rock, and I had to sing and everything. It was nuts."

Papa looked like he was about to interrupt, but Dad shushed him.

Sam sighed. "It was really cool. I mean, you should have heard some of these guys sing. And it's a pretty good

173

play. But—I mean—I'm not really a play guy. So I don't know."

Papa couldn't contain himself. "But what *is* the play? And did you get a big role? You've never acted before, but you've got a great voice, and your stories are terrific."

Sam sighed again, but he couldn't hold back a smile. "The play is *Annie*. And I just got a text from Ms. Daly. I got the part of Oliver Warbucks—the rich guy who adopts Annie."

There was a moment of quiet. Then everyone erupted again. Questions and congratulations came, loud and fast, and Dad started singing one of the songs that they all knew from their long car trips. Sam's smile grew even larger.

"That's just wonderful! Are you excited?" Papa asked.

Sam was quiet for a second, trying to figure out how to explain.

"The soccer tryouts are in the spring. And now I won't be able to make the so-called optional indoor practice schedule this winter. Coach Javi called it optional, but what if he only recommends players who go? I'll be totally nailed." Sam scowled.

"But there are open practices at the YMCA gym," Dad said. "I just got an email from Javi. I'm sure you can make a bunch of those, and between that and the skating on the rink, you'll be in great shape!"

Sam looked unconvinced. Dad and Papa exchanged looks.

"Is there anything else?" Papa asked.

"It's just . . . the play kids are all . . . you know," said Sam. He paused. This wasn't going to go well.

"Nope," Papa said.

"They're all arty, and they wear black jeans. And they all skateboard."

"You skateboard. Tyler skateboards too," Dad pointed out mildly.

"Yeah, but it's not the same!" Sam was getting frustrated. "None of them are like me! They don't play sports!"

"Are you sure?" Papa looked fairly skeptical. "I would think sixth grade is a little young for kids to stop all sports. What about the girl in your class? Emily?"

Sam blushed slightly. "She plays soccer. Central midfield."

Papa just raised his eyebrows.

"But most don't! Or at least, not seriously," Sam insisted. "And none of my friends are doing it, and there are more girls than boys, and I never hang out with girls. It's just different!"

Jax was nodding eagerly, like he wanted to help. He said, "It's just . . . regular kids don't usually do the play. Or at least boys. That's all."

Papa leaned against the doorframe. "Well, with all due respect, that's the silliest thing I ever heard. You're a great athlete. You have fun telling stories. You're doing the sixth-grade school play. As far as I can tell, this is just plain exciting! Anyone who doesn't think so . . . well, send them to talk to me. Is Tyler giving you a hard time?"

"No! Tyler's cool. He was just surprised, that's all. It's fine." Sam shuddered slightly. The only thing that would light Keith and those guys up more than Sam's being in the school play would be Papa's defending him for being in the play.

"Sam, different can be a good thing," Dad said. "It's good to get out of your comfort zone, to not be an expert at everything. For goodness' sakes! You're twelve—you're supposed to try new things. Just because you're excellent in soccer doesn't mean you shouldn't try anything new for the rest of your life."

Sam tried to smile, but it felt like a grimace. The thing was, he was really good at soccer. And he loved it. The more new things he tried, the better chance he had of completely stinking at them. And he really, really hated stinking at something. But still, the thought of turning down the part and watching someone else . . . No. No, it was his part. He wanted it, and he'd earned it. He smiled at his family, who were all staring at him. Even Eli had come in to see what all the fuss was about, but he was standing apart from everyone else, arms wrapped around himself. He looked so small and miserable that Sam was startled. Was his brother shrinking?

"Now!" Dad said, looking around. "Is there any other news we should know about?"

Frog leaned forward, eyes wide. "Ladybug's cat is having kittens. Can we get one?"

Before anyone could respond, Eli spoke up.

"I'm not going back to Pinnacle."

Sam sighed as everyone started shouting again.

Chapter Twenty-Two

IN WHICH ELI ENTERS THE BIG FREEZE

Dude, you are a hard man to track down. Seems like every time I call, Froggie tells me you're "unavailable." And we both know that means you're avoiding the phone.

Anyway, E-man, I just wanted you to know that I love you lots, and you can tell me anything. You can tell me why you won't go to school. You can tell me why it hurts to admit you made a mistake. You can tell me that you're worried that maybe you're not as smart as you thought. (Don't worry. You are.)

And if you feel like it, you can tell me why some brides say they want 450 white-chocolate buttercream cupcakes and then decide at the last minute that the cupcakes should instead be dark chocolate with raspberry fondant. If you figure that one out, let me know. And meanwhile, maybe plan a trip down to NY soon—I'll have 450 white-chocolate cupcakes in my freezer.

Love, Lucy

Eli wasn't talking. Not after his announcement, while his whole family yelled at once and asked questions and answered them and then asked more questions. And not now, in the car on the way home from Sam's celebratory dinner, with everyone in the van staring at him in the evening darkness that already looked like midnight. Eli could feel their eyes on him.

"When—" Dad began to ask, but Eli shut him down with a growl.

"When do play rehearsals start, Sammy?" Dad continued, pointedly ignoring Eli. "Do you have a schedule yet?"

Sam was peering at the glowing screen on his knee. "Yeah, Em texted it. Tomorrow there's an all-cast meeting, and then they're going to give out schedules through next month."

Dad had unearthed an old copy of the *Annie* sound track, and Eli couldn't help enjoying the songs. He even laughed out loud when his brothers gave their expected chorus of "It's the Hard-Knock Life," complete with added verses.

Papa, presumably encouraged by his laughter, asked, "Do you want to see if Ambrose can come home with you sometime this week? He might enjoy checking out the rink."

Eli stopped laughing like someone had turned off a switch. "I told you, I'm not going to school," he said.

In the dark car, Eli could see Dad shake his head slightly at Papa, but Papa, who was driving, didn't notice. Or at least he didn't pay attention.

"Eli, you've got to at least tell us what's up. Did something happen before vacation? Give us something to work with!"

Eli was silent.

"Something must have happened. What's going on? Did you argue with that boy—was his name Mika?—who told you our rink was an outrageous use of natural resources? Because if he gave you any more trouble . . ."

Mountains were no more silent than Eli.

"Well, is it the work? Is it too hard? Eli, you don't have to always get everything right. We can get a tutor and work with you if things are tough," Papa continued. The rest of the car had gone silent, the music sounding oddly cheerful in the background.

Eli made stone walls look chatty.

"Well, *heck,* Elijah! You can't just go mute! Either you plan to get your butt up at regular time tomorrow and get in the car with Dad. Or start talking!"

Frog spoke up. "Papa, you said a bad word! You owe us money."

Next to Eli, Sam winced. Frog's attempt to curb bad language rarely worked when Papa was in a mood.

"Sorry. I think that quarter already went to the Pinnacle School!" Papa said, snorting in frustration.

"Jason, enough!" Dad said, and his voice was loud in the quiet car.

Eli felt his throat close with tears that he really, really didn't want to shed. Crying would be the very worst thing to do right now. Mostly because he wasn't sure he would be able to stop.

He knew the school was expensive. His parents had explained the difference between private school and public school, and he understood, but had begged to go anyway. And they had agreed. This was his fault. There was no way he was going to tell them about it. A small sob escaped, and he bit down hard, wanting to make sure that no others followed. From behind him, he felt Jax's hand on his shoulder, but he didn't react. He didn't shake it off either. After a few comforting pats, it was gone.

When they arrived at the house, everyone unloaded silently. Sir Puggleton was ecstatic to see them and did his usual rolling-around-hysterically routine, but this time Eli couldn't be bothered to get down and roll around with him.

Without a word to anyone, Eli went to bed.

In the morning the Fletcher household was in an elevated state of chaos, the usual morning madness escalated by first-day-after-vacation challenges.

"Lunches are made! Just put them in your lunch boxes. Jax, make sure you pack a sandwich, not just junk. No, grapes don't count as a sandwich. Do they look like a sandwich? Eli? ELI! Where are you?"

From his room, Eli could hear Papa bellowing.

"Dad, where's my history book?" Now Sam was yelling as he clomped down the stairs. "I showed it to you on the first day of break. Where did you put it?"

There was a groan, then Dad's voice. "Sam. Seriously? I have no idea. We cleaned up for the holidays. I'm sure I put it carefully in a pile. Good luck finding it. I have no time right now. I've got a staff meeting and can't seem to find my interim reports. Where's Eli? Eli? EEEEEEEELIIIII?"

Still Eli sat in bed. Had they all forgotten? Did they not remember he wasn't going to school? His question was answered.

"Eli, I need you down here. We've got to get going!" Dad yelled up.

Eli swung his legs off the bed and reached for his slippers. Because of the chaos of getting out the door on school days, Fletcher Family Rules stated that no kid could come out of his room without getting dressed, but Eli didn't care. Defiantly he stormed out of his bedroom, his too small fuzzy pajamas a declaration of war.

When he got to the bottom of the stairs, the insanity of a Fletcher morning was even clearer. Papa was running around in his rocket-ship pajamas, his bathrobe flying behind him like a cape as he tried to stuff Dad's reports into his briefcase while holding a piece of cinnamon toast with the other hand.

"Frog! Your toast is ready—come eat! Leave the cat alone and get your toast!" Papa yelled toward Frog, who was on his hands and knees trying to tease Zeus with a laser pointer. Zeus looked bored.

Dad caught sight of Eli standing motionless at the bottom of the stairs.

"What's going on here? We need to be out the door in ten minutes, max! Are you still in your pajamas?"

"Duh," said Jax. He was standing in the kitchen doorway shoveling oatmeal into his mouth. "Did you ask if he was wearing his pj's? Of course he is!"

"It's called a rhetorical question, moron. That's a question that you already know the answer to," said Sam.

"Why would you ask a question when you already know the answer? That's just stupid," Jax retorted.

"Both of you, *quiet*. NOW." Dad sounded serious. Jax reapplied himself to his oatmeal in silence.

Eli really, really didn't want to talk, but he knew the silent treatment could get him only so far.

"I told you," he said finally, not looking at Dad. "I'm not going to school." His whole body was clammy. He hated this.

"Are you sick? What's going on?" Dad asked.

Eli shook his head. He wasn't going to lie, wasn't going to pretend his stomach hurt. But he wasn't going to school. He couldn't.

"I just can't," he said, and to his horror his voice cracked. He didn't want to cry.

Dad looked over at Papa, who was now madly shoving lunchboxes into the boys' backpacks. Then he looked back at Eli.

"Fine. Fine. You stay home today. I'll phone the school on my way in and let them know. You'll be keeping to yourself while Papa works. We'll talk about this tonight. Maybe you just need a reentry day." He turned away and started pulling on his winter coat and hat.

Soon he was gone in a blast of cold air and a puff of exhaust that almost hid the car as it sped out of the driveway. Moments later Jax and Sam left for their walk, bundled in scarves, hats, and jackets.

It was just Papa, Frog, and Eli. In the sudden silence that was left, Eli couldn't help feeling nervous. What had he done?

Papa turned to him. "Look, Eli, I get that something's going on here. You haven't been yourself for a while now, and Dad and I have been worried, but we figured you'd talk in your own time. Now you're refusing to go back to the school you said you loved, but you're still not talking. So you can take today to figure this out, but you have to tell us what's going on. Deal?"

"I guess," Eli said dully. But how could he tell them he'd made the biggest mistake of his life?

Later that day, as Papa fielded work call after work call, Eli wandered outside into the damp winter air. He stood, leaning against the side of the hockey rink, staring into the gray snow-filled sky. There was no color anywhere.

Suddenly the door next door opened and Mr. Nelson stepped out, his red flannel shirt making a bright spot in the dullness as he walked to the edge of the porch. He scowled when he saw Eli, and stormed across the yard to the edge of the low shrub that separated their properties.

"You! I've been meaning to talk to your parents. If there is any more harassment, I *will* call the police. And that's a promise!"

Eli blinked. "What harassment?" he asked.

"Let's see. . . . Since I moved in there have been flowers with bees in them in my mailbox this fall. Skunk bait on my porch. Garbage left by my door. And that doesn't even include the damage your soccer balls do to my garden. Don't think I don't have proof, because I do." Mr. Nelson seemed to be working himself into a frenzy. "I don't know what's wrong with you kids, but I'm telling you clearly that the next time, I'm calling the cops."

"But—" Eli didn't even know how to begin. How

could he ever explain about Jax's attempts at diplomacy? "We didn't know there were bees in the flowers. And that wasn't garbage—they were Christmas presents. We were trying to be nice! Jax wants to talk to you—"

"Nice!" Mr. Nelson barked a nasty not-funny laugh. "What's nice about having a bunch of wild kids targeting your house? What kind of stupid idea was that?"

Eli didn't answer. He couldn't. Just now, every single idea he'd ever had felt stupid. He blinked back tears.

Mr. Nelson regarded him balefully for a moment, but when he spoke his voice was slightly calmer. "What are you doing home? Didn't school start back up?"

Eli shrugged, trying not to cry. "It did. But . . . I didn't go today."

Mr. Nelson scowled more. "You sick? Or just playing hooky? Wouldn't be surprised if your parents didn't even believe in school . . . if they just taught you using the Google or something like that."

Eli didn't know what to say. Of course his dads believed in school. *He* believed in school. But somehow Pinnacle wasn't what he wanted anymore. And he didn't know how to say it. He curled his arms tighter around himself.

"I'm not playing hooky," he mumbled. He wished Mr. Nelson would just go away.

Mr. Nelson, however, was still there. "Why are you hanging around, then? You sick?"

Eli shrugged. "I don't . . ." He trailed off. Then his voice got stronger. "I don't like my school. At all."

Mr. Nelson laughed his not-funny laugh again. "Oh, really? That's a reason for kids to skip nowadays? Figures. Your brothers all home too? They don't like it either? Or is it just you?"

Eli's face was hot, and he was starting to get mad. "They don't go to my school, okay? They have no idea what it's like there. Their school is fine—they have friends there, and nice teachers. My school . . . Well, I thought I wanted to go there, but I hate it. People aren't nice, and they don't let us talk during lunch, and even though I thought the work would be really interesting and it kind of is, it's not worth it. I won't go back!"

Mr. Nelson's eyes bugged a little. Eli realized this was probably the most he'd ever said to Mr. Nelson.

"Huh. Must be nice to have a choice. Your brother left me a note that he wants to interview me for some Veteran Project. Well, I don't know when I'll have time for that kind of nonsense, but I'll tell you this: those kids in Vietnam, they'd consider themselves darn lucky to have even one school they could get to without walking for days on end. And here you are whining about your choice of two—"

"I have no choice!" Eli shouted. "I already chose this school!"

"Well, choose back, boy!" Mr. Nelson said, almost as

187

loudly. "You didn't get drafted to that school, did you? Just choose again, only different this time!"

Eli paused, his mouth open to tell Mr. Nelson he couldn't. He knew, even as he was about to say it, that Mr. Nelson would ask why not. And he didn't have an answer. Instead he said, more quietly, "There are some cool things. I did a research project on what makes bridges stay up, and even tried to build one. Out of cardboard and stuff." His heart lifted a little at the memory of the project. Despite the visit to the principal's office and the forced apology to Mika, he had gotten an "exemplary" grade, and it still felt good to remember it. "It was pretty cool, actually. I learned about the first suspension bridges, and about spans, and . . ." He trailed off.

Mr. Nelson looked . . . Eli couldn't think of how to put it. Mr. Nelson looked sad, almost. But he turned away.

"Well, that's more useful than most airy-fairy stuff they teach nowadays." He walked to the mailbox on the side of the porch and grabbed his mail. "Now. I want your word that you won't go trying to be 'nice' anymore. I don't want the noise, the animals, the pests, *nothing*. Got it?"

Eli nodded once, and Mr. Nelson slammed back into his house.

Left alone again, Eli went back inside. Twenty minutes later there was a knock at the door. When he went to open it, no one was there. But lying on the mat, wrapped in a plastic grocery store bag, was a big, gorgeous, hardcover book. *The Brooklyn Bridge: A History of Engineering* read the title, and underneath, it said "by Silas H. Nelson." Stuck to it was a Post-it note that read:

Don't mess up this book. I want it back. —SN

Chapter Twenty-Three

IN WHICH JAX IS AT A LOSS

Dear Tom and Jason,

Jax has done some really excellent research on his Veteran Project, but he seems a bit unwilling to dig into the interview. I've tried to get a sense of what the problem is, but he seems unhappy when I bring it up.

While the final project isn't due until the spring, it is important that he keep on top of it. If you have any concerns or additional questions, don't hesitate to call. Otherwise I'll assume that Jax will be back on track soon.

Sincerely,
Ms. Sugarman

It was a pretty awesome weekend, Jax thought, except for the *Thing* in his backpack. He'd managed to ignore it during the Friday Chinese-food-and-movie night, and hadn't even thought about it as they'd raced out the door to his indoor soccer game on Saturday morning. But now it was Sunday afternoon and they were all hanging around. All was normal except for the Thing. Well, normal if having Sam texting Em and laughing goofily was normal. And if Eli's still refusing to talk about what happened at Pinnacle was normal. Eli had spent the past week staying at home with Papa during the day, doing worksheets and reports that Papa scanned and emailed to the school. Jax had no idea what they had told Eli's teacher. There had been some whispered grown-up conversations and phone calls with Pinnacle, and all Jax knew was that his brother was still at home. Whenever Jax tried to ask him why he wouldn't go back, Eli would clam up. So it wasn't that normal, really. But still.

Gloomily he wandered over to where his backpack was hanging on a hook. Dad and Papa were both in the living room, watching football with Sam and Frog. Frog mostly liked the dances the cheerleaders did, but the rest of the family were huge fans. The New England Patriots were winning by a mile, a fact that Jax hoped might help his parents ignore the Thing.

After walking back into the living room, he waited until there was a particularly exciting play, then thrust a folded piece of paper into Papa's hand.

"Here, Papa," he said, hoping his voice sounded casual.

"What's this?" Papa asked, not looking at it.

Jax shrugged. "Just a note from Ms. Sugarman," he said.

Unfortunately, the game went to commercial break at that moment. Papa looked down at the paper, opened it, and read. When he was done, he handed it to Dad.

Jax stared down at the rug. There was a faint stain where Sir Puggleton had once barfed after eating an entire apple pie. The thought of apple pie barf pretty much matched his mood. He tried to find an animal in the shape of the stain.

When Dad was done reading, he looked up at Jax. Jax stared at the barf stain. Maybe a camel? He kept looking.

"Jax, do you know what the note says?" Papa asked. To Jax's misery, they hadn't even noticed that the game was back on.

Jax nodded.

"So what's going on? You said you had an extension and didn't need to start the interview, I thought."

"We did have an extension. Until last week." Jax kept staring at the floor. Not a camel. Maybe a wolf . . .

"So what happened? I thought you were excited about this project?" Dad asked.

Jax didn't answer. The fact was that he *had* been excited. The more research he did, the more cool stuff he had found. Mr. Nelson had been in Vietnam when the city of Saigon surrendered to North Vietnam, he had flown helicopters to rescue South Vietnamese families who'd wanted to leave, he had been given all kinds of awards, and he'd gone on to design helicopters and other stuff for the military. *Then* he had gone into civil engineering and helped with roads and bridges. Jax had even—not that he'd ever show anyone—made up a pretend interview with Mr. Nelson.

"Jax?" Papa prodded.

Jax finally looked up. "I've done a lot. And found even more articles on the Internet. Stuff about the war, and about how Mr. Nelson rescued people, and how the Americans left. I just haven't written it down yet. But you know he told Eli that he didn't want to be bothered and he'd tell me when he was ready. And he never even answered the note I left at Christmas. And I tried to go with Eli when he went back to return the bridge book, thinking maybe he'd be willing to at least set a time, but no one answered, even though his car was there. So we just left the book and Eli's thank-you note by the door. I just . . ." He trailed off.

"You just what?" Dad asked.

Jax was silent for a moment. Then he burst out, "He's scary! He's so grouchy, and he yells at us all the time, and in the article I read there were these gross pictures of dead people. I don't know that I want to talk to him. Henry's report is practically done. His cousin sat in a computer lab somewhere in Egypt and wrote code, as far as I can tell."

Dad and Papa exchanged a long look. Jax twisted a

corner of the couch pillow until it wouldn't twist any-more. His stomach felt queasy, and he didn't think it had anything to do with the leftover tacos he'd had for lunch. He just didn't want to do this. But he didn't want to mess it up either. The thought of his project in the newspaper flitted in, then back out of his mind. Why had he chosen Mr. Nelson?

Finally Dad spoke up. "It sounds like you're not that far behind. And I'm impressed with all the research you've done. So let's try to get some parts of the report done based on that, and then you can show Ms. Sugarman. And now that it's time for the interview, Papa and I will help try to get that set up. It might be time for advanced diplomatic action."

Jax let go of the cushion and watched it unwind. He felt a little better. Maybe with Dad and Papa helping it wouldn't seem so scary. For a moment he let himself think again about his report in the paper, of sending it off to Lucy and his grandparents, of Ms. Sugarman an-nouncing him as the winner during morning assembly.

At that moment Sam gave a bellow, and all three of them turned back to the television.

"What? What happened?" Dad asked, leaning forward to see better.

Jax leaned forward too but stopped as Papa put a hand on his back.

Jax looked up at him. "I'll work on it after the game, okay?" he asked.

Papa nodded. "That's fine. But I just wanted to tell you that we're proud of you. This assignment shouldn't be easy. It should make you think, and you're doing a great job."

Jax felt a warmth spread over him, and he smiled, what felt like the first real smile since the Thing had come home with him. Papa hugged him, and Jax snuggled in. The Patriots were still winning, and things were looking up.

Chapter Twenty-Four

IN WHICH ELI CAN TOLERATE 81 DAYS

Dear Eli,

Papa is helping me write this note because I asked him why you weren't going to school, and then when he told me you didn't like it anymore, I wanted to write to you. So I am writing to you to say I am sorry you don't like it. I love my school and Ms. Diane, and I think you should go to a school you love too. Jax likes his school, I think. I think so because he comes home happy and he plays with me after school, not like you, who used to come home mad and didn't ever want to play. Anyway, I hope you are happy again.

Love, your brother

Frog

It was turning into the weirdest winter ever, Frog thought. Eli hadn't gone to school for more than two weeks, although he kept doing his schoolwork at home. When Frog tried to ask his parents why Eli didn't have to go to school, they just told him Eli was going through a rough patch. Frog wasn't sure what that meant, but it didn't sound good. Meanwhile, Sam was forever quoting his lines for the play, saying things like, "Tell the president I'm busy," or "I think you'll find it a very fair price!" and using different accents each time. And Jax was always trying on the new shirts he had gotten for Chanukah, though he never seemed to actually wear them. Frog was glad that he at least got to ride the bus. That was about the best thing going these days.

"The days are getting longer," Papa said one afternoon as they were walking home from the bus stop. As was becoming the new normal routine, Eli had come too, and was walking ahead of them now with his head down, kicking at clumps of ice and snow as he walked.

Frog looked up. It was cold out, and between his scarf and hat he couldn't hear very well. "What did you say?" he asked.

Papa pulled up one side of his hat so his ear was exposed. "Days. Getting longer. Moving toward the spring equinox," he said loudly.

Frog pulled his hat securely back down over his ears. "It sure doesn't feel like spring," he said.

"Nope, it sure doesn't. But look down toward the harbor. See the steeple? After vacation the sun was already at the top of the steeple when I picked you up from the bus. And look at it today. It's a good ways above it. Days are getting longer, all right."

Frog glanced at Eli. He knew Papa was only partly talking to him. Frog had heard both Dad and Papa, and even Sam—and Lucy, on the telephone—trying to talk to Eli. But when Eli went silent, boy, he was silent. Frog wasn't surprised that he never answered any of them. Finally they seemed to just let him be. But the whispered grown-up conversations that stopped as soon as he came into the room still went on. Frog hated it. He just wanted Eli back to normal.

"How many school days are left?" Frog asked.

"Eighty-one," Eli said.

Frog's eyebrows disappeared under his hat in surprise that his brother had answered, and he turned to Papa, his mouth already open to ask questions. But Papa spoke first.

"That sounds about right," Papa responded. "I know we're more than halfway through the year. . . . Dad was celebrating."

Eli didn't say anything. Frog looked anxiously from one to the other. Papa went on.

"Of course, there are vacations too. We'll be going to Florida to see Great-Grandpa Opa next month, and there's the winter carnival. Then Grammy and Grandpa are coming up for Easter and we'll do the big hunt on the green. Oh! Let's not forget the Holi festival, too. That's coming up. And we'll do a Passover seder. . . ." His voice casual, Papa painted a picture of a train of good times, one car following another all the way to summer.

"Then it's going to be nice out! And we'll get the kayaks into the water, and go catch snakes and turtles. . . . Froggie, remember that tiny baby turtle we found last year? It was the size of a quarter."

Frog nodded.

They walked in silence for a few minutes. Frog was dreaming of turtles, which of course made him think of kittens, and he was surprised when he heard Eli again.

"If I finish this year at Pinnacle, can I go to Shipton Upper Elementary next year?" Eli asked, still kicking at ice.

Frog was confused. Weren't they talking about turtles?

"Papa, can I—" Frog started to ask.

"Absolutely," Papa answered, his voice loud and warm.

Frog beamed. "I can? Really? That's the best thing in the whole world! I love you so much, Papa!" he cried, throwing his arms around him.

Eli and Papa both looked at him.

"What the heck are you talking about?" Papa asked, looking down at Frog, who was hanging on to him like a large limpet.

"I guess I can stand eighty days," Eli said, although he wasn't really talking to anyone.

"You are the best Papa ever!" Frog said, hanging on tighter.

"What's going on here!" Papa asked, prying Frog off him. "Eli, did you agree to go back to school for the rest of the year?"

"You said I could get a turtle! And I've wanted one forever! I really, really, really want one!" Frog yelled, exultant.

"Yes!" said Eli.

"NO!" said Papa.

"What?" said Frog and Eli at once.

"What do you mean, no?" Eli said, his scowl building again.

"Yes!" Papa tried again.

"Thank you!" Frog yelled.

"Stop. Everyone, just . . . stop."

They stopped, despite the fact that they were half on and half off the sidewalk, ready to cross the street. A car slowed to let them pass, then honked in annoyance when they ignored it. They stepped back onto the sidewalk.

Papa spoke slowly. "Eli, you can certainly change back to Shipton after this year. That isn't a problem. I am very proud of you for sticking out the year and seeing it through." He paused for a second. "Frog . . ." He hesitated. "I didn't really say you could get a turtle. I'm sorry, buddy. It's just that with Zeus and Sir Puggleton . . ."

His voice trailed off. Frog knew Sir Puggleton wouldn't care about a turtle, and Zeus would be interested only if it were crawling around on the floor.

"Um . . ." Papa looked trapped.

He glanced at Eli, who had forgotten to kick the ice and was looking up in interest, clearly wondering how this was going to end.

Papa threw up his arms. "What's one turtle? Sure, Froggie. This spring we'll get a turtle. Just for you!"

Frog whooped and tried to high-five Eli. Eli high-fived back and even smiled.

Frog looked back at the harbor one more time before they finally crossed the street. "You're right," he said, grabbing hold of Papa's hand. "The days are definitely getting longer."

Chapter Twenty-Five

IN WHICH PLAY PRACTICE TAKES OVER ALMOST EVERYTHING

> **Em cell:**
> Today's rehearsal was AWESOME! Thx for your address—I'll come by after school today or tomorrow to run lines. What do u think we should do for that peanut butter dance scene? Oops. Parenthesis dance. PARTNER dance. Stupid phone. Anyway, any ideas?

"Which way sounds better?" Sam asked. He stood up a little straighter, then said, "I should think *so*!" in a loud, deep voice.

"Now compare it to this," he said hurriedly in his real voice. Then he stood up straight again. "I should *think* so!" he said in the deep voice again.

Tyler just stared at him.

"Well?" Sam asked, impatient. The play was coming

up, and he still wasn't sure which sounded better. The six weeks of practices since winter vacation had been cool, but mostly they'd made him realize how really, really badly he didn't want to stink. Not in front of the whole school.

"Um . . . they both sounded fine," Tyler said finally. "Dude, you're all crazy arty these days." He shook his head and laughed a little.

"I'm not!" Sam was indignant. He was going to at least three soccer practices a week, even if he had to sprint there from play practice. He was still playing football at lunch, ignoring Emily when she wanted to run lines. What more did he need to do to convince Tyler he was still himself?

"Whatever. Hey, do you want to come over for pizza after soccer tomorrow? My mom said she'll pick us up at the Y and we can hang at my house for a while."

Sam's shoulders dropped. "Um . . . I can't. Play practice." He refused to call them rehearsals.

Tyler looked resigned. "Dude. Like I said . . . arty. Anyway, I've got to go. See you later." He shouldered his backpack and started to walk.

"Wait!" Sam called. "Do you want to come over now and skate? It's supposed to get really warm this weekend, so this is probably our last chance before the rink dies."

Tyler looked back over his shoulder and shrugged. "Sorry, man. I told Keith I'd come over after school. See you tomorrow."

"See you," Sam said. He sighed. He and Tyler had barely gotten any time on the rink this year. He had heard at school that some new family who lived near Keith had built a backyard rink too. Probably Keith and Tyler were over there while he was at play practice.

When he got home, he went to find Jax and Eli. "Want to get a little skating in? It's going to be melted soon."

Jax jumped up immediately, and after a combination of pleas and threats, Eli agreed to come out too after he finished his cursive sheet.

Sam and Jax sat on the mudroom bench, lacing up their skates.

"Any chance Hen is coming by?" Sam asked. "We could use a fourth."

Jax shook his head. "Nah," he said. He stared down at his laces, but Sam could see his brother's eyebrows scrunched up and his lower lip sticking out. Clearly something was up.

Now that Sam thought about it, Henry hadn't been around much. In fact, Sam wasn't even sure if he'd been over since Thanksgiving. It wasn't like the old days, when Henry had been in their house practically as much as Jax.

"What's going on with him, anyway?" he asked Jax. "You guys still cool?"

"Kind of. I guess. But he's always busy, either with

indoor lacrosse or playing over at Ian's house. And now he's supposedly 'going out' with Jessica, which means they eat lunch together. It's stupid." Jax kept pulling at his laces, even though they were plenty tight. "And he's always wearing some dumb shirt or hat or something, like it matters! Suddenly he's all about being cool!"

Sam nodded understandingly. Henry wanted to be cool, and hanging out with Jax didn't seem to qualify. He thought for a minute about Tyler, who had barely been over all winter, and wondered if all the Fletchers were going to end the year friendless. Shaking his head to get the idea out of his brain, he clapped Jax on the shoulder hard and offered him a hand.

"His loss, bro, if he's acting like that. He'll come around. But for now, let's skate! I'm feeling the need to kick your butt!"

Eli, Sam, and Jax blasted up and down the ice, slamming the puck back and forth between them. Sam let loose a snap shot that made a noise like a cannon when it hit the boards. He grinned.

The three of them played in the late afternoon light, which lasted longer than it had just a week ago. Sam had just faked out both his brothers and flipped the puck over the boards and was taking a mock bow, when he heard clapping.

"Bravo, bravo!" came a voice from the driveway.

Sam put his arms down and skated over to the side. Squinting into the sun, he saw it was Emily.

"This is *so* cool!" she said, looking at the rink in amazement. "I can't believe you never mentioned this!"

Sam ran his hand over his sweaty face. His brothers stared at Emily as though she had horns growing out of her head. He glared at them.

"Um . . . yeah, I didn't know you cared much about skating. Do you, like, figure-skate or something?"

Em wrinkled her nose. "Figure-skate? No! I grew up playing hockey, and I still play with my brothers sometimes. I played Mite and Squirt, but when it was time for Pee Wee, I gave it up—I decided I'd rather do soccer. And plays."

Sam raised his eyebrows. "Really?" He tried, and failed, to keep the amazement out of his voice.

"What? Don't I look like a hockey player?" Em grinned. She was barely up to his shoulder, and looked like she weighed about as much as Eli.

"Well . . . to be honest . . . not so much," Sam said, and laughed.

"What size do you wear?" Jax interrupted. "I have huge feet. Maybe you can wear my old skates. We need a fourth."

Sam smacked Jax on his helmet. "Shut it! Like Em wants to wear your old stinky-butt skates. You're such a tool."

"Sure!" Em said. She actually looked excited. "I'd love to! But do you have an extra helmet? Ms. Daly would *kill* me if I come in with a black eye. . . . I don't think that's the look she wants for Grace Farrell."

Once the skates and helmets were on, they faced off, two on two.

"Easy, Jax," Sam muttered to his brother as they lined up. "I don't want you to hurt her."

Jax nodded solemnly. Seconds later Emily streaked by him and put the puck perfectly on Sam's stick, and they were up by a goal. Five goals later, and Sam called a halt. He could tell by Jax's expression that losing five to zero was *not* okay. He looked about ten seconds from a Vesuvius-sized blowup.

"Okay, let's switch it up. Jax and Em, you're against me and Eli."

Em grinned at him. She knew exactly why the teams were changing.

"Hope you like losing, Sammy," she said, and the game began again.

By the end of the game, they were all dripping with sweat, and it had ended with Em and Jax winning by a goal.

"You're pretty good," Em said, offering her hand to Sam to shake. "You might even beat me someday!"

"I should think so!" Sam said in a deep voice. And this time it sounded absolutely perfect.

Chapter Twenty-Six

IN WHICH JAX IS WITHOUT A BEST FRIEND

To All Fletchers with Opposable Thumbs:

We are hosting Celina and Cam tomorrow night for a relaxing evening of grown-up conversation and fine food. It is my goal that the house not resemble a baboon pit the night after a wild party. Actually, even baboons probably don't leave several days' worth of mud-encrusted clothes by the stairs.

Please deal with said items, as well as anything else that is filthy, wet, muddy, or just not where it belongs. (And yes, Eli, that definitely includes mealworms in a container that looks like Chinese takeout left on the dining room table. . . . That was nearly a harrowing mistake for Dad last night.)

I will begin lurking near the stairs to offer encouraging reminders in the afternoon.

Love, Papa

The rink was a thing of the past, and mud season had officially begun. Normally it would have been one of Jax's favorite times of year, with soccer starting up and he and Henry getting ready to terrorize the soccer league. But this spring he had barely seen Hen. He'd come over once, when Amelia had called Papa to see if Henry could hang out one evening. It had been almost like old times; they'd been playing and joking and teasing Zeus, but when she had come to get him, it had been weird all over again. It wasn't all bad; he saw more of Ronan and Miles and Derek, who also played soccer and lived nearby. They were cool guys, but it was different from Hen.

And meanwhile, he still hadn't interviewed Mr. Nelson. Dad had gone over to talk to him, but had come back kind of grim-faced, saying that Mr. Nelson was really busy and he'd call when he had time. Dad had talked to Ms. Sugarman, so Jax wasn't in trouble. The research he'd been doing at school, along with the timeline of the war and the poster he was making, was pretty cool. But he sure wasn't going to get his report in the paper if he never even got to do the interview.

At least they finally had outdoor recess again. There had been an almost record-breaking number of rainy days, and Jax thought that if he had to spend another minute in the cafeteria trying to play quarter hockey without getting yelled at by the lunch monitors, he would go nuts. Today was awesome—a T-shirt day—and he couldn't wait to get on the playground. Maybe he and Henry would be captains of the football teams, like they used to be.

On the way outside to the playground, Jax's excitement grew. It was a perfect early spring day, the drip, drip, drip of melting snow coming from the whole long roofline of the school, and excellent muddy puddles everywhere but the dry blacktop. He ran toward the back corner where the football crew always met.

"Hey! You guys want to make teams?" he started to ask. But the words died away as he heard Henry's voice, loud and harsh. His back was to Jax as he leaned on the pole for the basketball hoop.

"It's so freaking lame, you guys. I mean, you wouldn't believe it. I had to go in there to get my water bottle the other day, and they were, like, dancing and prancing about! Like a bunch of tools. I was embarrassed just watching them. Then Sam saw me and waved. I was like, 'Dude, stop tap-dancing like my little sister!' Seriously! Keith was peeking through the door, and we were cracking up."

Jax was hot and cold all at once. Was Henry—could he be talking about Sam? His Sam? His brother, who Henry had always thought was the coolest person in the world? And since when was Henry so buddy-buddy with the sixth-grade guys? He sure wanted everyone to know it.

Jax stayed silent, hanging back. He didn't know what to say.

Ronan spoke up. "You're kind of harsh, H. I mean,

Parker does the play every year, and he's, like, the funniest guy in the school. And he's a sick baseball player."

"Yeah," someone else said. "I thought the play last year was pretty funny. Remember that talking plant?"

There were some murmurs of agreement.

But then someone said, "Yeah, but . . . dancing? I mean, seriously, Hen, they were dancing?"

"Yeah, like, in a line. Like this!" Henry did a goofy cancan dance, kicking his legs up in front of him.

The group laughed a little. Finally, an ice age later, Ronan saw Jax.

"Yo, Jax, we playing? You brought the ball, right?"

Jax looked at the football clutched in his hands. He had forgotten he was even holding it. Suddenly he was so mad, it felt like red ants were biting him all over his body, all at once. He whipped the football as hard as he could at the back of Henry's head. It hit with a satisfying thwack, then bounced to the ground.

"HEY! That hurt! What the heck is wrong with you, moron!" Henry shouted, turning around in a hurry.

"Moron! You're the moron! Bragging about hanging out with Keith and trashing my brother! He'll always be cooler than you. At least he's trying something new! What have you ever tried? You won't even play basketball because you're not good at it! You're a pathetic jerk!"

At this, Henry launched himself at Jax, shoving him backward in the chest.

It took around two minutes for the recess monitors to

cross over and separate them, but it was the longest and most miserable two minutes Jax had ever spent.

They were marched to the principal's office, both sweaty and muddy from where they had rolled off the pavement. Jax was trying desperately to blink back his tears of rage. He wanted to keep hitting Henry. He wanted to wipe that smug laughing look off Hen's face so hard that it could never come back.

The principal, Ms. Morris, had other goals.

"I have no idea what happened, and I'm not asking, so don't tell me. Instead, I'm going to tell you something. I'm sure you both feel you have a reason for fighting. And you might. But you deal with that reason on your own time. After school, you can talk it out, punch it out, never speak to each other again . . . that's your choice. But in this school you will *never, ever* hurt another student. Got it?"

The boys both nodded. Jax stared at the pattern on the rug. It looked kind of like the one in Papa's office. Oh, how he didn't want to have to tell—

As though she were reading his thoughts, Ms. Morris continued. "I'll be calling your parents right about now. And while I'm doing that, you can go sit with Dr. Clarke and talk to her about what's going on here."

The time in Dr. Clarke's office was endless. She reminded them about zero tolerance for violence and that they needed to talk through their problems, but Jax wasn't listening, and judging from the way Henry was staring at the door, neither was he. Jax kept staring at him, hoping he would look guilty, or sad, or even apologize for saying such stupid things about Sam. After all, it wasn't like they had never fought before. They'd fought plenty. . . . Henry had even given Jax his first black eye when the joking tickle fight they'd been having had turned rough.

But Henry didn't look sorry, or sad. He looked mad and distant, like he wanted to be anywhere but here. Well, Jax couldn't blame him for that. At least his stupid fancy dark jeans were ripped. That was something.

When Papa burst through the door, all three of them jumped, even Dr. Clarke.

"Mr. Fletcher!" she said, getting to her feet. "Glad you could get here so quickly. Jackson will have to leave school with you for the day. As you know, we have a zero tolerance policy—"

"Yes, I know, I know," Papa said. "And I certainly agree violence is not the right answer, especially in school."

His eyes raked over Jax, taking in his ripped shirt, muddy pants, and whatever expression a face has when one's best friend has been shown to be a backstabbing moron. Then Papa looked at Henry, who wouldn't meet his eyes.

"Let's go. We'll talk at home. Dr. Clarke, I'll be in touch," he said, offering Jax a hand.

As they walked out of the room, Jax couldn't help looking back one last time. But Henry was still staring in the opposite direction.

They were in the car before Papa spoke again. "I suppose I should be grateful that Eli at least went back to school. There's a limit to how much truancy and suspension I can deal with in one time period." He sighed. "Now, do you want to tell me what happened?"

Jax wanted to explain it. He wanted to show how stupid and lame Henry was for making fun of Sam because of the play. He wanted to tell Papa that the other kids knew the play was cool, even if the dancing was kind of weak. But all he could say was "Henry's not my best friend anymore" before the tears started to fall. And as they drove home, with Papa's comforting hand reaching back to rest on his knee, Jax felt that really, there wasn't anything else to say.

Chapter Twenty-Seven

IN WHICH SAM'S HONOR IS DEFENDED (BY A MOST SURPRISING PERSON)

> Sam,
>
> Here's your costume, clean and hemmed. PLEASE BE CAREFUL CARRYING IT TO REHEARSAL! Ms. Daly will not be pleased if you hit it with a muddy soccer ball. Again.
>
> Love, Dad

Soccer season was starting up, and Sam was dirty. Really dirty. It wasn't his fault; the fields were especially muddy this year, with the late thaw and the heavy rains. And normally it wouldn't be a problem, except that mud was the difference between being able to make it to both soccer practice and play rehearsal on time, and being late. Once, he had tried to just towel off the mud and head straight to the auditorium, but Ms. Daly had taken one look at him and sent him home to shower.

The rehearsals were sick. Sam was constantly amazed at how good the other students were. He had never known his classmates could belt out songs, or fall totally into a character. And Ms. Daly was pretty cool too. She kept talking about the evolution . . . of the play, of each character, of who the audience thought you were at the beginning and who they thought you were at the end. There was always tons to think about.

Now, having showered the mud off, Sam was on the verge of being late for rehearsal. Again. He knew Ms. Daly would be mad. But he wasn't going to skip practice—he just couldn't! Already Coach Javi had made some comments to the team about how effort counted as much as talent. Never mind that Sam was making more of an effort than anyone else he knew, running between practices and play rehearsals. And it wasn't like anyone on the team cared about the play, or vice versa. He had learned to keep each one in its place.

The clocks had sprung forward, and it was not dark out yet. Sam knew he should probably take the road, since Papa couldn't give him a ride. But it was easier and faster to cut straight across the back woods by Mr. Nelson's and go through the convenience store parking lot. He glanced at his watch. Ten minutes. Starting to run, he headed into the dimness of the far yard. It was the first full dress rehearsal, and he had his costume—a freshly pressed tuxedo, tailored to fit—in a white plastic bag on his shoulder. He entered the woods at a slow jog.

"Where you going, fancy pants?" said a voice from the trees.

Sam stumbled and nearly fell. "Whoa, you scared me! Who's there?"

"I said, where are you going?" the voice said again, and this time several other people laughed.

A bunch of shapes moved out of the shadows to stand in front of him, in a loose semicircle. Sam looked around. It was a group of boys who looked like they were in high school. They were smoking cigarettes, their flannel shirts and blue jeans barely showing up in the dim light of the burning cigarette tips.

"What do you want?" Sam asked, trying to sound bored and wishing he hadn't been so startled. Papa had always told him the key to not being bullied was to seem uninterested and unafraid. He wasn't sure it was working. His heart was still pounding from the run, and now he was uncomfortably aware that the boys were moving closer.

"Don't be rude, punk!" one of the boys said roughly, putting a hand out to stop Sam from walking farther. "My friend here asked where you're going. Answer him."

Sam sighed and glanced at the convenience store parking lot through the woods, where the lights shone brightly. But he and the group of boys were too far away for anyone at the store to see them.

"School. Okay?" Sam said. "I've got to go back to school for a . . . practice." He had almost said "rehearsal," but he knew that would be a bad idea.

"Yeah? Why you going back to school now? Aren't little boys like you supposed to be home after school?" the same boy asked.

"Mikey, ask him what's in the bag," another voice said.

They were still standing in a circle around him. Despite himself, Sam couldn't help being nervous. He glanced behind him toward Mr. Nelson's backyard, but several of the boys were behind him now.

He didn't say anything.

"Hey! Punk, I asked you what was in the bag," said the one called Mikey.

Sam felt a flash of annoyance. "Actually, you didn't ask me. Your dipwad buddy told you to ask me. But you never did."

He knew it was a mistake the minute he said it.

As quick as a flash, the bag was ripped out of his hands and torn open. The white shirt shone like neon in the dim light.

"Woo-ooh! Isn't that adorable? You got a date? Go on, punk, tell us all about it!" crowed Mikey.

Another one grabbed the blazer from his friend's hand and dropped it onto the ground.

"Oops," he said, stepping deliberately into the middle of the fabric. "Looks like you might want to wear something else." He dropped his cigarette onto his muddy boot print and carefully stomped it out. "Yeah, not looking so good!"

"Give it back!" Sam yelled, forgetting to be scared. He shoved through the group and bent down and grabbed the jacket. A quick kick to his back sent him sprawling through the dirt and rotten dead leaves.

As their laughter echoed around him, Sam stood up and ran back to Mr. Nelson's backyard. Tears of rage were streaming down his face. He was practically a teenager! Things like this weren't supposed to happen!

Blinking through his tears, he paused when Mr. Nelson's sensor light came on, blinding him. Perfect. Now he was going to get yelled at. This night reeked.

"What the heck is going on here?" came the voice from the back door. Sure enough, Mr. Nelson was peering out, looking as crabby as ever. "Who's there?"

Sam was getting really sick of being asked that.

"It's me, Sam Fletcher," he said, trying to shield his eyes from the powerful flashlight Mr. Nelson was shining in his face. "Sorry, sir. I was just trying to . . . I mean, I cut through your yard because I was late getting to school."

"What? You're going the wrong way. And why are you still here, then?" Mr. Nelson had stepped off the back porch and was coming closer. "If this is another one of your so-called nice acts, I swear I'll call the cops. I've had enough of your family's harassment! You can tell your brother that I don't have time right now for some fool interview. I'll tell him when I'm ready."

"No, it's nothing like that." Sam sighed. "I ran into a group of—"

"And why on earth are you so filthy?" Mr. Nelson continued, cutting him off. "Who did you run into?"

There was a moment of silence while they looked at each other. Then:

"TROUBLEMAKERS!" Mr. Nelson hollered. "They hang out around here far too much. Far too much! Sometimes I find their darn cigarette butts in my yard. Did they do this?" he gestured at Sam's mud-spattered state.

Sam nodded.

"That's unbelievable. UNBELIEVABLE! That's the last straw. Hooligans." Mr. Nelson turned back toward the deck and grabbed something off the stairs.

"Now, let's go. Show me where they are." He started at a fast walk toward the woods. Sam watched Mr. Nelson's bandy legs and bedroom slippers disappear into the trees before he came to his senses and ran after him. He glanced back once at his own house, where he would love to be, getting Papa or Dad to deal with this. But he couldn't let Mr. Nelson go alone.

"Mr. Nelson! Wait! NO! Mr. Nelson, stop! There were a whole lot of them. I don't think . . ." He trailed off in astonishment.

Mr. Nelson was facing off against the boys, who had now started to pass around a bottle.

"You little ferrets!" Mr. Nelson was yelling. "You're not welcome in my backyard! You're probably not welcome in your own backyards either, but that's not my problem. Now clear out!"

"Hey, old man—" one of the boys started.

But Mr. Nelson swung toward him. His whole posture had changed, and now he stood, ramrod straight, his everyday flannel shirt and camouflage jacket suddenly taking on a military bearing. Sam had never realized how tall Mr. Nelson was. But now, standing there, staring down the high school boys, he looked . . . menacing. Sam was suddenly aware of all the war stuff Jax had been telling them. Mr. Nelson had faced down worse than these guys. Sam was glad to be on the same side as the former soldier.

"Quiet, you! I'm not done." Mr. Nelson took one step forward, and the boy shut up.

"Now. Any of you punks decide this is the best place to cause trouble, plan on meeting me here. This is MY backyard, and I choose who goes through here. A bunch of lazy bullies who gang up on younger kids . . . NOT WELCOME!"

There was a moment of silence, then Mr. Nelson nodded. "Good. Now get outta here."

Mr. Nelson was breathing heavily, and Sam had a

panicked moment of wondering if he was going to have a heart attack. But no, he was standing strong, the few hairs standing up on his balding head backlit by the bright porch lights.

The boys swore, shuffled their feet a little, but, eyes down, melted away toward the convenience store parking lot.

Then Sam was alone with Mr. Nelson.

"I . . . uh . . . Thank you," Sam said uncertainly, bending down to grab the ruined suit. He wasn't sure that his pathetic thank-you was worth much.

"Huh. Didn't do it just for you. It's ridiculous to have my own yard terrorized by a bunch of little ferrets." Mr. Nelson didn't sound any more pleasant than usual.

"Okay . . . Well, I guess I'll . . . um . . . go home and tell my dads now," Sam said. Forget being late. By the time he showered and got a ride, he'd be lucky to get there at all. He'd better text Em to tell Ms. Daly the news.

"You want to take this with you next time? Just in case?" Mr. Nelson held out the item he had grabbed from the porch. In the dark, Sam hadn't even noticed it. It was a crowbar, large and dangerous.

Sam gulped. The thought of his grumpy neighbor madly swinging a crowbar was terrifying. "Oh! Um. No, thank you. Thanks for offering, though."

Mr. Nelson grunted and moved back toward his house. The last thing Sam heard before he got home was Mr. Nelson saying clearly, "Little ferrets."

His heart was still beating uncomfortably fast, and his costume was pretty much ruined. Oh, and he was going to miss rehearsal and was again covered in mud. But Sam was smiling. He couldn't wait to tell Em about the evolution of Mr. Nelson.

Chapter Twenty-Eight

IN WHICH FROG GETS A KITTEN AND A LADYBUG

Mr. Nelson,

Sam told us what happened last night, and Jason and I want to thank you. Truly, for all our disagreements, you acted like a real neighbor and we are grateful. Many thanks again for looking out for our boy.

Best, Tom Anderson

P.S. Also, Jax was wondering if you by chance had any time for his interview next week. He has to turn in the project at the end of the month. He's also eager to show you the work he's done so far.

"It's Family Night tonight! Don't forget. Dad? Daaaad? It's Family Night. Hey, Sam, you're coming, right? It's Family—"

"Night. Got it," said Dad, dropping a kiss on Frog's

head. "We all got it in the book, Froggie. Wouldn't miss it for the world."

"I would," said Eli gloomily. "Why on earth do I need to go to a kindergarten open house? It's so boring. All we're going to see is Frog's stupid cotton-ball bunnies and math workbook."

"Because we all went to yours, and we were mightily impressed with your cotton-ball bunnies, once upon a time," said Papa as he handed Jax his breakfast. "And now it's Froggie's turn."

"You can see where Flare sits when I have work. And you'll *finally* get to meet Ladybug. And her moms. They're all coming. Her rash is all gone. She was allergic to stuff. Her oldest sister will be there. She's in seventh grade. But her middle sister can't come. She has some rehearsal or something."

"I thought she had three sisters," Jax said.

Frog shrugged. "That was wrong. There are only two. She made up the third."

Jax rolled his eyes.

"And that's another thing," Sam said. "I know it's not my rehearsal tonight, but I really should go anyway. Just to . . . you know . . ." He paused, clearly trying to think of a reason he'd need to be at the rehearsal even though it was only for the orchestra.

"Nice try, Sammy," Papa said, handing over a plate with four eggs and three pieces of toast. "You'll come check out your brother's class with the rest of us. Just like we'll all be at your opening night next week. The Family Fletcher—"

"Fights finks and forest fires!" said Jax.

"Finds freedom!" intoned Sam.

"Frees frightened frigid foxes from ferocious finks with fangs!" Dad said triumphantly.

The rest agreed that Dad won, and breakfast proceeded with no more discussion.

When it was time for the family to go to Frog's class, they all trooped down the street in the last fading daylight. Frog gave them a running commentary on the sights and sounds of his bus ride.

"Here is where Isabelle gets on the bus," he said, gesturing to a corner. "And sometimes Jimmy gets on with her, but usually he refuses. Once, he got on the bus, but he had a rubber snake in his mouth and the driver made him get off. Most days his mom drives him. One of the teachers calls him Feral Jimmy. What does 'feral' mean?"

The brothers walked on, mostly ignoring Frog. He didn't care; they were coming to his classroom!

Inside Ms. Diane's room, all was chaos. The Peace Loft in the corner was filled with older siblings, one of whom was pretend-shooting his orange Nerf gun over the side. Frog hissed in disapproval.

"We're not supposed to have weapons! AND there's only one person allowed at a time up there." He looked around the room. "And no one is supposed to touch Mr. Blue," he said, pointing to a blue-tongued skink that was being enthusiastically handled by a toddler.

"Let's just enjoy your work, okay, buddy?" said Dad, drawing Frog in from the doorway, where he was staring around like a tiny indignant principal.

With a few interested questions about colorful maps—and, yes, cotton-ball crafts—Frog was back to being excited. All six Fletchers were crouched in the corner near the cozy mat and pillow nest where Flare slept, when a tiny voice right over the low bookshelf made Frog jump.

"Frooog! You're here!"

As his brothers watched, a tiny girl came barreling around the bookshelf and hugged him tightly. "Why are you so late? Are these your brothers? Where are your dads? Mom brought the kitten in the car—you guys can take it home tonight!"

Frog shot a worried look at his family. The kitten! He had never actually gotten permission, although he was pretty sure he had asked. He just couldn't remember the answer. The family was staring, mouths open, in astonishment at the nonstop chatterbox.

Sam was the first to recover his voice. "What kitten?" he asked.

At this point a tall woman with a dark suit and a blond bun stepped into the corner. It was getting very crowded.

"Are you the Fletchers? Ladybug Li has talked so much about your son! I'm Carol Johnston, one of her moms," she said with a wide smile. "I'm *so* sorry we haven't been able to get the kids together yet this year. With everyone's schedules and Li being sick so much—turns out she has wheat and dairy allergies. Well, you know how it is. Anyway, delighted to meet you now." She held out a hand.

Papa shook it automatically, looking baffled. Frog beamed up at him.

"See?" he said proudly. He was proud of his friend, from her red Chinese jacket that she wore for special occasions, to her tight braids, to her missing three front teeth. She was missing more teeth than anyone else in the class except him.

"We've certainly heard a lot about your daughter too," Papa said, shooting Frog's brothers a warning look.

But Jax apparently didn't notice. "We thought Frog made her up! We didn't really think there could be a girl named Ladybug with two moms and three sisters in the same class as a boy named Frog with two dads and three brothers! We've been telling him he's a moron all year! Boy, are we dumb!"

He turned around and gazed at his brother and Ladybug reproachfully, as if it were their fault he'd thought Frog was lying.

Frog was astounded. They hadn't believed him! He turned to his fathers. Dad was still trying to get past Jax, Sam, and Eli, who were now lying right in front of where Papa and Carol stood.

"Dad, Papa, you knew I was telling the truth, right? You were trying to call Ladybug's mom to see if she could come over, I thought." He was silent for a moment. Then his face darkened. "Weren't you? Did you just say that?"

Carol was looking from family member to family member, perplexed.

Dad spoke. "Froggie, it's just that there was no one in the phone book or school directory with the last name "Li." And the phone number you brought home didn't work. And she wasn't at Grace's birthday party. And you know, with Flare and Shaman, and Connecticut, your baby brother . . ." He trailed off.

Frog looked indignant. "That's different! I'm not DUMB! But Ladybug is in my class. I told you that."

Carol waded into the fray. "It sounds like there was some confusion. 'Ladybug Li' is my daughter's first name. Well, really it's 'Li,' but her sisters call her 'Ladybug Li' or just 'Ladybug.' Her real name is Li Johnston-Fischer. We're in the school directory, but not the phone book because—"

"You're Judge Johnston," Papa said. "Of course! I knew you looked familiar. There was that big interview with you in the *Boston Globe* last month."

"No wonder we couldn't find her under *L*," Jax muttered.

Frog gave him a look. During this entire frustrating exchange Ladybug had been babbling on, trying to tell him about her latest drawing, which was on the art wall. Shooting one last glare at his family, Frog let her pull him away.

Dad, who had by now negotiated around the boys, shook Carol's hand. "Well, this is all very funny. Carol, I'm Tom Anderson, and this is Jason Fletcher, and of course Sam, Jax, and Eli, Frog's brothers."

Carol smiled. "Sam, I've heard all about your performance. My daughter Sara is a clarinetist. She's at rehearsal tonight."

Sam gaped. "Sara is Ladybug's sister? But . . . I see her every day, practically." He looked baffled that Frog's imaginary world had such mundane roots.

After all the revelations, the two families chatted, and it turned out that Sara played soccer with Olivia, and that both families spent summers on the same remote beach on Rock Island, only during different months. Frog, who had wandered back over, couldn't stop grinning. His friend had *finally* met his family. And they all got along.

Just as Ms. Diane was ringing the bell for circle, Carol turned to Dad. "So, you ready to meet your newest family member?"

Dad looked confused, and Frog paused, stricken.

Right! The kitten! Well, hopefully they'd remember he *had* actually asked. Even if they never listened.

"Your kitten! I brought her all cuddled up in a blanket in a carrier in the car. She's all ready for you. I hope you're ready for her. She's a little spitfire! I found her crouching on the molding around the stairwell the other day, like a furry orange gargoyle."

"Kitten," Dad said cautiously. "Um . . ."

To Frog's endless relief, Ms. Diane rang the final bell. "Quiet, please," she said. "It's time for the kindergarten-ers to sing their special song."

As Frog began to sing, he couldn't help looking over at Dad. He was whispering something in Papa's ear, and Papa was looking resigned. Frog sang a little louder and felt Ladybug nudge his foot with her own. It was turning into the best Family Night ever.

Chapter Twenty-Nine

IN WHICH MR. NELSON COMES TO DINNER

> TO: PAPABEAR
> FROM: JUDGE JOHNSTON
> SUBJECT: PLAYDATE
>
> Jason, it was great to finally meet you. We'd love to have Frog (and the kitty) come for a playdate some-time next week, so just let me know what works for you. Also, I'm terribly sorry about the confusion—I really thought you wanted a kitten. But hopefully you'll enjoy her once you get used to her.
>
> Best, Carol

When Jax got home from school, there was an ambulance in front of the house, lights flashing, and a police car right behind it. He started running.

"Papa!" he shouted as he burst through the door. "Frog? Is everyone okay?"

Papa emerged from his study, his face perplexed.

"Frog's at Ladybug Li's house. And why wouldn't we be okay?"

"There's an ambulance outside," Jax said, panting. Clearly he had run for nothing. "Is something wrong?"

Papa walked over to the door and looked out. "Must be next door." He slid his feet out of his slippers and into his flip-flops and opened the door. Jax followed him out.

Outside in the chilly spring sunshine, all was wild activity outside Mr. Nelson's house. A fire truck had pulled up behind the police car, and a knot of uniformed people were huddled around talking. Jax wished Frog were there; he wouldn't want to miss a fire truck right by their own house.

Papa shook his head. "This doesn't look good," he muttered.

As he spoke, the uniformed people moved out of the way, and a bunch of EMTs came out of the house carrying a stretcher. Mr. Nelson walked behind them. They didn't seem to be in any rush, and there was no sound except for the burst of static from someone's radio. The person on the stretcher was completely covered—even the head.

Jax peered more closely as they put the stretcher into the ambulance and then pulled away.

"Why aren't the sirens on?" he asked Papa.

Papa sighed and turned to him, pulling him close in a

one-armed hug. "Because, my sweet son, there's no rush anymore. That person—"

"He was DEAD?" Jax asked loudly. He had never seen a dead person before. Even covered up. It was creepy. But also kind of cool.

"Shhhh," Papa said gently. "Yes, the person is dead. And it was someone who lived with Mr. Nelson, and he must be very sad right now."

Jax considered this for a minute. After Mr. Nelson's heroic defense of Sam with the crowbar, the Fletchers had not seen much of their neighbor. He had been largely absent this spring, and mostly they'd been grateful to avoid his muttered threats about footballs killing his roses. He had ignored Dad's last message about the Veteran Project, and Dad and Jax had made an appointment to talk to Ms. Sugarman about what he should do to complete the assignment if he couldn't interview his veteran. Jax had taken to drawing pictures of Mr. Nelson being hit by lightning, or attacked by aliens, or other punishments worthy of ruining his project.

Papa had started talking to one of the other neighbors in a low voice. Jax inched closer to listen to Nancy, who knew everything in the neighborhood.

"I guess he had been taking care of her for the past ten years or so, but she really went downhill last year. That's why they moved here—the house has a first-floor bedroom and bath, and we're only ten minutes to the hospital. He wouldn't let her go to a nursing home or anything. She was ninety-six years old, and hadn't spent a day in the hospital, or so I heard," Nancy was saying.

"Mr. Nelson's wife was ninety-six?" Jax asked, amazed. That was really old . . . almost one hundred.

"No, honey. It was his mom," Nancy said. "She had been living with him since she'd gotten too frail to live alone. It's an awful lot of work to care for someone like that. But Silas never wanted any help." She shook her head. "It's going to be an empty house for him, I'm afraid."

Jax walked away, but he couldn't get his mind off Mr. Nelson. He had been taking care of his mom all this time? All those days when he'd yelled at them to be quiet, maybe she'd been trying to nap. Or maybe she had felt sick. Jax remembered visiting Great-Aunt Helen in the hospital, how she had moaned and whimpered in pain and how much it had scared him. Had old Mrs. Nelson been in pain like that? And now Mr. Nelson was all alone in that big empty house. Jax suddenly felt bad about all his mean revenge drawings. He wished the diplomacy had worked.

That night at dinner, Papa and Jax told the rest of the family what had happened that day. Jax could see his brothers struggling with the information. Mean, grumpy Mr. Nelson was suddenly a person whose mom had died. Eli spoke up.

"Remember when he loaned me that book about the Brooklyn Bridge? That was pretty neat." He kept eating, but he looked thoughtful. Since returning to Pinnacle, Eli had seemed more cheerful, though Jax noted that each night before bed he put another big red X on the calendar that counted down the school days.

"And you should have seen him that night in the woods!" Sam added. "Honestly, those punks just melted away. He's one tough dude. Even without a crowbar."

"Do you think he wants to come over and see the kitten?" Frog asked. Lili, the new kitten, was poised on the arm of his chair, staring greedily at his fish dinner, while Zeus waited patiently below for Frog to drop something. "Kittens are good for cheering people up."

Papa exchanged a glance with Dad, who said, "Well, when he first moved in, we went over to introduce ourselves, and . . . well, he wasn't particularly gracious. And he certainly let Jax down on this project. But maybe it's time to try again."

To everyone's astonishment, that Saturday, Eli offered to go over with Jax and ask Mr. Nelson to come to dinner. The rest of the family watched breathlessly from the kitchen window as the boys bravely walked through the yard and knocked on the door.

When Mr. Nelson answered it, he looked like he was going to yell for a second. Then he just looked tired.

"Come to do that darn interview? Fine. I'll do it. But it better not take more than ten minutes," he said.

Jax and Eli shook their heads vigorously. "No! No, that's not why we're here," Eli started.

Jax interrupted. "We just wanted to invite you to dinner."

Mr. Nelson shook his head. "I don't want dinner. And I don't want a lot of bother. I just—"

"I wanted to show you my bridge model," Eli said, and Jax could tell he was getting nervous. Eli's voice always got squeaky when he was nervous.

"I don't need to see some lousy bridge model. I've seen enough bridges to last me a lifetime," Mr. Nelson said, trying to shut the door.

Eli's cheeks were a hot red, and he looked like he was trying not to cry.

But Jax wasn't about to cry. Jax was mad. "It's not lousy, actually," he said. "It's awesome. Eli makes the coolest stuff ever. He designs it from scratch and builds it. And I know you designed stuff too—sick stuff like lighter helicopters and special pros . . . pros . . . fake legs and arms and stuff! And that you even got awards for it.

But I bet it wasn't any better than Eli's models!" He was breathing hard.

"And I know you saved all those people in Saigon, and that you got special medals for it. But here in Shipton you're not exactly very nice." Jax shut his mouth with a snap. Now he'd done it. He'd insulted a grown-up, and a grown-up whose mother had just died! He was afraid to look up.

After what felt like a year Mr. Nelson cleared his throat, and Jax glanced up, wincing. He didn't want to be yelled at. But at least Eli no longer looked like he was going to cry.

Mr. Nelson coughed. "Well. Maybe I wasn't very polite." He paused for a minute.

"Tell your folks to expect me at seven," he said. Then he went back in and shut the door behind him, quite quietly, Jax noticed.

"He's coming," Eli reported when they got back home. "At first he didn't want to, but Jax kind of motivated him, I think."

Papa gave Jax a funny look but didn't ask any questions, for which Jax was deeply grateful.

"Did you tell him about the kitten?" Frog asked.

"I forgot," Eli said. "But he'll see her tonight."

"I'm sure Lili will cheer him up," Frog said confidently,

but Jax wasn't so sure. He was nervous. What would they say to once-grumpy-now-tragic Mr. Nelson?

When he arrived later, Mr. Nelson seemed more grumpy than tragic, to Jax's relief. He muttered a hello to Sam and Jax, ignored Frog, and gruffly handed Eli another book. Papa and Dad quickly handed him a drink and brought him into the dining room.

"Will you be working in your garden at all this spring?" Dad asked politely once they were all sitting down.

"No. Only did that for Mum," Mr. Nelson responded tersely.

Silence fell.

"Are you still consulting on building projects?" Papa asked.

"Not if I can help it. Sometimes the fools call me when they can't get anyone else stupid enough to work with them," Mr. Nelson said.

Another silence. Jax was beginning to sweat.

Slowly the conversation started up again around the table, this time without attempting to include Mr. Nelson. Sam told about the final dress rehearsal coming up for the play, and the cast party they had planned on a sailboat someone was renting. Eli mentioned an email he had gotten from Anna at the farm. But Jax couldn't help staring at Mr. Nelson. It was too weird, having him here, knowing he was all alone, knowing all the heroic things he had done. . . .

"What the devil are you looking at, son?" Mr. Nelson barked, startling Jax out of his reverie. "You've been staring at me since I got here! Do I have fangs? Or horns coming out of my head? Well, do I?"

Jax choked and nearly spit a bite of roast chicken across the table. His face felt hot as everyone in his family turned to stare at him.

"Jax, is there something you want to say?" Dad asked softly.

Jax was silent, fighting embarrassment. But to his surprise he realized there was something.

"I just wanted to tell you I'm very sorry that your mom died," he said finally. "That's really sad. And . . . well . . . I'm sorry it happened. . . ." He trailed off lamely. He winced slightly, waiting for the explosion.

But Mr. Nelson was silent. His eyes were shiny, and for a horrible moment Jax thought that Mr. Nelson would burst into tears. But he didn't. He reached over and patted Jax heavily with one hairy, calloused hand.

"Thank you, Jax," he said. He paused as though he would say something more. But he just looked around the table, where the other five Fletchers were all looking back at him. "Thank you," he repeated.

Papa caught Jax's eye and smiled. "Mr. Nelson?" he asked. "Can I interest you in more potatoes?"

Mr. Nelson nodded and took the platter, and the noise picked up again. Soon Mr. Nelson was lecturing Eli about the Golden Gate Bridge, and Sam was quizzing Frog on addition problems, and Dad was complaining to Papa about the new report cards at his school. But Jax knew something had changed. Now Mr. Nelson had really joined them for dinner. Finally diplomacy had worked.

Chapter Thirty

IN WHICH ELI AND AMBROSE DISCUSS MATTERS

TO: ANNABANANA_HAS_A_FARM
FROM: ELIFLETCHER1
SUBJECT: BRIDGES
Hey anna—thanks for your email. I love the picture of the baby goats. They're so cute!!!!!!!! Guess what? Im going back to my old school and this summer my aunt lucy is going to take me on some special tour of the brooklyn bridge! I will take lots of pictures.
Eli

He did love the new kitten, Eli thought as he watched Ambrose sneeze another five times at the desk in front of him. But it was unfortunate that his only sort-of friend at Pinnacle was so allergic that the fur on Eli's clothes made him sneeze, no matter how much Eli tried to clean himself off before school. Of course it didn't help that Lili preferred to sleep in Eli's shirt drawer more than anywhere else. When he shut it tight, Lili would sit and yowl until he opened it again. So all his shirts were pretty fuzzy.

Ambrose sneezed again, just as Ms. Gallwin was excusing the class for a fifteen-minute "oxygen and energy break."

"Sorry," Eli said to Ambrose as they half walked, half ran toward the door together. It was a spectacular spring day, and fifteen minutes might not be long, but it was better than nothing. When they got outside, Ambrose pretended to sneeze onto Eli's head, which had Eli chasing him around the Physical Activity Space, which had Ambrose tripping him onto the grass so that they both went down in a tumbling pile.

Eli couldn't remember the last time he had laughed so hard at school. Actually, he wasn't sure he had ever really laughed at Pinnacle. The thought made him sigh.

Ambrose looked over. "What's wrong? Boogers in your hair making you sad?" He started laughing again, which made him sneeze, which just made him laugh harder.

Eli smiled, but the laughter had been chased away. "Nah, I'm just thinking about school. . . ." He hadn't told Ambrose yet that he wasn't coming back. When he'd come back after winter break and Ambrose had asked where he'd been, Eli had just told him he'd been sick. Now, with only one week left of school before their summer break, he had to explain that he wouldn't be back. Not for summer term, not for next year, not ever.

"What are you doing for break?" Ambrose asked. "And guess what? I heard we're doing a beach day with environmental science curriculum sometime during summer term. Isn't that excellent? There's no swimming, of course. I don't think we can even take off our shoes and socks, actually." He was silent for a second, but then he cheered up again. "But still, it'll be cool going out to Rocky Point. There are crabs there."

Eli hadn't heard about beach day, but he didn't care. He didn't want to spend one day on the beach, not allowed to take off his socks and shoes—how lame was that? He wanted to spend the whole summer on the beach the way they always did—burying each other, putting crabs in Papa's sneakers, bodysurfing the tiny waves that rolled up onto the shore. He cleared his throat.

"That sounds . . . um . . . cool. But, actually, I'm not going to be around." His voice got quieter.

"What? Dude, you know my ears are stuffed up. What did you say?" Ambrose sneezed again.

"I'm not going to be here. Not this summer. Or . . . um . . . at all. I'm going back to my old school," Eli said, a kind of relief flooding him as he said it out loud. Still he felt bad. Would Ambrose be mad? Did he feel like he was being abandoned here, at this miserable place?

Ambrose stared at him, his mouth agape. Eli could see his nose starting to run, but felt it wasn't the right time to mention it.

"Ambrose? Dude, I'm—" Eli started.

"Seriously? But WHY?" Ambrose sounded shocked but, Eli was relieved to note, not mad. "It's awesome here!"

It was Eli's turn to look shocked, but he tried to hide it. Awesome? How . . .

"I mean, at your old school, didn't they get all hyper over recess, and spaz out and beg the teacher to show movies, and throw things in the cafeteria? I thought you hated it there," Ambrose said.

Eli didn't know what to say. He had hated those things. Or at least, he'd thought he did. Now, though, he was kind of excited to get back.

"Not everyone was like that," he answered, shrugging. "But . . . yeah, some are. A lot, actually. But . . . I don't mind, I guess."

He thought back to Anna's words at the farm. "You can learn whatever you want, whenever you want, but at your new school you get credit for it and at your old school you didn't?" she had said. Eli thought about it now. He could still research why bridges stayed up, or why platypuses were still considered mammals despite laying eggs, or what a degenerate red dwarf planet was in astronomy; no one was going to stop him.

Ambrose was going on. "But here no one goofs off in class. And the teachers aren't scared that you'll be smarter than them. And nobody teases us for being brains. And the library is actually quiet. And—"

Eli cut him off. "No, I know. Really. It's a cool place.

It's just . . . I like my old school. I miss it." As he said it, Eli could feel himself relax. It was that simple.

Ambrose shrugged but didn't look upset. "I don't get it. You'll be back in a class where no one wants to do anything. But . . ." He shrugged again. "Whatever, I guess."

They sat silently for a minute. The warning bell had already rung, letting students know they had five minutes until recreation time ended.

"Hey!" Ambrose said suddenly. "Maybe you can come over after school sometime this week! And this summer can I come to your house? I can't go inside, you know, because of the cats, but maybe we can play in the yard."

Eli grinned. Maybe, just maybe, he had made a friend. Even if he never came back to Pinnacle School after next week, he would have that.

Chapter Thirty-One

IN WHICH SAM GETS A STANDING OVATION (AND JAX DESERVES ONE)

To Jax and Sam—
Unless you feel like paying the $89.45 that we owe in lost library books, I suggest you start looking for them. The long-suffering school librarians are threatening to break your kneecaps if you don't return the books before the end of the year. (Okay, they're really just threatening to withhold your report cards, and, Sam, not let you graduate from sixth grade, but still.) Please look everywhere, no matter how vile. Sam, that means your soccer bag.
Love, Papa

Sam's opening night was the end of the civilized world. Or at least that's what it felt like to Jax. Both Papa and Dad had taken the day off work in order to watch the dress rehearsal, then taken Sam out to lunch, and now were running around the house yelling at everyone to get into the car already, curtain was in twenty minutes. Thank goodness Aunt Lucy and Mimi and Boppa weren't coming until the weekend, Jax thought. It was already too crazy to handle.

"It's, like, a two-minute drive!" Jax protested, as Dad sent him upstairs to change into non-muddy pants and told him to HURRY UP ALREADY.

"Jason, do you have the flowers?" Dad called.

"I took them out so they would open. They're right—AHHHHHH! Stupid moronic kitten! Where is that idiotic . . ." Papa's voice trailed off, and Jax knew he was desperately trying to swallow the swears that were building up.

"What happened?" Jax asked eagerly. He rushed down the stairs in clean jeans, hoping Dad wouldn't send him back up for fancier pants. It was a school play, for goodness' sakes.

"She didn't mean to," Frog was protesting, cuddling Lili closely. The kitten's mouth was stained red, and for a horrible minute it looked like she was drooling blood. But then Jax realized it was flower petals.

"Well, shoot. How many did she eat?" Dad asked, joining them to study the damage.

"There are still enough. It's just not a very large bouquet," Papa answered, glaring at the kitten. She began

248

making desperate hacking sounds, then promptly threw up on Frog's shirt.

"EWWWWWW!" Frog yelled, dropping Lili.

Jax burst out laughing, even as he danced out of the way of the red-tinted cat barf.

It was another ten minutes before they were out the door.

They got into the auditorium just as the student volunteers were closing the doors. With much shuffling, shoving, and whispered conversations about who was going to sit behind the tall dude in the row in front of them, the five Fletchers finally got themselves seated. Mr. Nelson, who had come earlier to save them seats, gave them a spectacularly dirty look as they rustled in, but they ignored it. Mr. Nelson had been around a lot lately, first for the interview that Jax had started the day after he'd come for dinner. But more and more he was just coming over to bring yet another book for Eli, or to see if Jax had finished the report. To everyone's astonishment but Frog's, Mr. Nelson had also taken a great liking to Lili the kitten, and could be found dangling bits of yarn or a tiny toy mouse that he'd brought over with him. And despite his comments at dinner, he was seen digging out in his garden again, grumbling at the weeds.

As the lights were going down, Jax took one last look

around him. He gulped and quickly faced the stage again. Sitting directly behind him, his knees touching Jax's seat, was Henry, sitting with a bunch of other fourth graders.

The play began.

As the music swelled (with Ladybug Li's sister in the orchestra) and the actors took the stage, Jax couldn't believe how nervous he was. He couldn't imagine what it would be like to be Sam, actually waiting to go on and sing in front of all these people. Jax resisted the urge to turn around and glare at Henry. Why was he even at the play? Was he coming just to laugh at Sam and make fun of him with his new buddies? Jax shook his head impatiently. Henry wasn't worth bothering with anymore.

In spite of Henry, in spite of the boy in the orchestra who sneezed and knocked into his cymbal in the middle of a scene, and in spite of the occasional loud whisper from Frog, Jax was drawn into the play. And before long, Sam was striding out in a tuxedo, his hair slicked back and a cigar in his hand. He looked . . . cool. He was loud and important, and made everyone laugh with his jokes; he seemed to look right at Jax and wink; and, best of all, everyone clapped like mad when he went offstage. Jax glowed with pride. This was his brother! Jax felt exactly like he did when they watched Sam's soccer games and people would whisper about his amazing saves. Sam really was the coolest guy he knew.

When intermission came, Jax had to run to the bathroom, and by the time he got back, Henry was standing in the aisle talking to Ronan, Miles, and a bunch of other kids from their grade. These guys were all sitting together toward the back, their families nowhere to be seen. Jax was suddenly sorry to have Frog kneeling on a pile of coats next to him on one side and Eli, nose buried deep in the science book he'd brought for intermission, on the other. But Ronan waved.

"Yo, Jax. It's pretty sick, isn't it? Sam's so cool!" he said.

Jax waved back, a grin spreading over his face. "Yeah, he's doing pretty good," he answered.

" 'Well,' " Dad corrected automatically, then winced. "Sorry."

The boys hated having their grammar corrected in front of their friends. But Jax had barely noticed.

"Hey, come sit with us," Miles said. Henry had disappeared up the aisle a few minutes earlier—probably, Jax guessed, to grab as many Airheads from the snack booth as he could. Jax was about to ask Dad if he could switch seats, when the lights dimmed. With a sigh he sat back down.

The play continued, with Annie looking for her real parents, and Miss Hannigan and her evil brother trying to kidnap her, and Oliver Warbucks and Grace getting lovey-dovey, which was totally embarrassing to watch, and finally, the grand finale. It was awesome.

When it ended, everyone stood up and clapped. Jax pounded his hands together until his palms burned, then stomped his feet to make more noise. Papa let loose his wild New York taxi-calling whistle, and Dad did his hockey game "Woot, woot," and everyone else cheered. When Sam came out alone to take his bow, the crowd went even wilder. Mr. Nelson let out a holler like a moose that made the people in the rows all around them jump. There was a huge roar from Tyler and the rest of the soccer team, as well as the Fletchers. Papa looked like he was trying not to cry.

Eli turned to Jax, his glasses sliding down his nose and his cheeks pink.

"I think I might want to try out for the play. You know . . . just the chorus or something! That was so cool!" he yelled over the cheers.

Jax looked up at Sam, who was being handed two huge bouquets of mixed flowers, and who turned and handed one of them to Emily, who was bowing with him. She stood up on her tiptoes and kissed him on the cheek as a thank-you, and the crowd cheered even louder.

Before he could answer Eli, Jax felt a hand on his shoulder.

"Hey, dude," Henry said, his voice embarrassed. "I just wanted to say—no hard feelings, okay? Sam did awesome."

Jax's eyes traveled from Henry's embarrassed face to

the cheering crowds. He knew that Henry wouldn't have been making up with him if all the kids in the school hadn't been cheering Sam, calling his name and making him come out for a second, then a third, bow. Dad was right—Sam was brave. No matter what.

He took a deep breath.

"Sure, no hard feelings, man," he said, and put his fist out for Henry to bump.

Henry broke into a grin. "Great. So . . . maybe I can come over sometime or something?" he asked.

Jax shrugged. He was pretty sure that he and Henry would never be the kind of friends they had been before. But he didn't say so. "Yeah," he said. "Maybe sometime."

And he turned back to cheer on his brother some more.

Chapter Thirty-Two

IN WHICH WE SAY GOODBYE FOR NOW

TO: LUCY_CUPCAKE
FROM: PAPABEAR
SUBJECT: LAST DAY PHOTO
Hey, Luce—

So here it is—the last day of school. I'm not gonna lie—I cried at Froggie's moving-up ceremony, I cried at Sam's play and at his sixth-grade graduation, and frankly, I cried after I took this picture. They're good boys, our boys, and they're growing so fast. Come up soon, Luce—before you know it, summer will be over.

Love—your bro

"Take the picture already! Frog is sweating on me," Sam said through his smile. "And he stinks like turtle. It's gross."

"I do not!" Frog protested. He was holding Birdy, the turtle he and Papa had caught the weekend before. Birdy peed with great frequency, so the truth was that Frog did smell a bit, but he didn't care.

"Whatever. Just go," Jax said. He was itching to get moving. While he hadn't won the Veteran Project prize, he had been an honorable mention, and his name was going to be in the morning announcements with the other winners.

Eli was the only Fletcher not in a rush. Pinnacle School had ended a week earlier, giving its students a small break before summer term began. But it would begin without Eli. . . . He was free. Free to build a model bridge over the puddles in the yard, free to sit and read books about the Arctic for as long as he wanted in the tree house, free to play soccer in the backyard as soon as his brothers got home.

"Aaaaand . . . I got it!" Papa finally said from behind his camera lens. He looked up and smiled. It was a ridiculously, gloriously, perfectly sunny spring day. The plum tree in the yard was covered in flowers, the grass, such as it was, had returned, and all the Fletcher boys were in shorts and T-shirts, scraped knees and pale legs (for Sam and Eli) the hallmark of the early warmth.

"I'm off! Eli, I won't forget the Chinese food on the way home," Dad said.

"Last day of school meal tonight! And can we have a campfire after?" Frog asked, carefully putting Birdy back into her tank. "With marshmallows? And even s'mores? And can Sam tell us a scary story?"

"Can we set up the tent and sleep outside?" Jax added.

The others set up a cry, even Sam, who figured scary stories would sound even better in a tent.

"Can Em come over for the campfire?" Sam asked, his cheeks a little pink.

Papa looked over at Dad, whose classes had ended the day before, and who was going into his own school in shorts and a T-shirt. They grinned.

"Why not?" Dad asked, smiling at the boys.

"Why not?" echoed Papa. "After all, it's summer. Summer is just beginning."

Jax couldn't stay still any longer. Running across the yard, he kicked a soccer ball as hard as he could.

"Doofus! That's my ball!" Sam said. "And it's going to hit Mr. Nelson's grandiflora roses. You know he just mulched those last weekend."

"Oops! Sorry. I'll get it after school," said Jax. "Mr. Nelson won't mind if it's there for now."

"You better. I love that ball. It's even better than the orange one."

Their voices drifted down the street. And with the knowledge that campfires, s'mores, tents, and the story of the pet cemetery were all waiting, the family Fletcher headed out for one last day. Summer was beginning. It was almost here.

ACKNOWLEDGMENTS

There are two groups of people I need to thank: those who helped make *The Family Fletcher* into a book, and those who—through their own shenanigans—inspired the story.

First, there would be no book if the superagent Marietta Zacker had not found these wacky boys in her in-box and decided to give them a chance. Marietta has been a champion and cheerleader. She is wise in all things, from the value of pants[1] to karaoke, not to mention her wealth of publishing knowledge and know-how. There is no one I'd rather be buckled next to on this wild ride.

Marietta also gets massive points for bringing me to Delacorte Press and into the experienced and savvy hands of Michelle Poploff, editor extraordinaire. Michelle won my heart when she said the story had "Furniversal appeal"—a comment that doesn't make much sense now but at the time was spot-on (trust me!)—and she has helped make it better and better. I am so grateful for her guidance and insights. She also works at the speed

---

1   Trust me, we should all be grateful for our pants. Just ask her kids.

of light, and it is entirely possible she has superpowers, but you never heard me say so.

Long before the Fletchers were introduced to Marietta and Michelle, many patient people helped me roll the rock up the hill[2] again and again. I'm not sure this book would exist without the generous and encouraging online writing community, including Liz Whelan, Helene Dunbar, Marilee Haynes, Laura Tims, and the krakenworthy Alina Klein. These talented writers help pummel my work into shape, and they are excellent at making sure I remember to add a plot and that I don't overuse the em dash.[3] They also write really amazing books and let me read them first, which is awesome. Further, the LBs (a Super Sekrit Writing Lair)[4] are the best of the best at celebrating and commiserating the world of writing . . . I'm lucky to have found my tribe.

I also owe enormous gratitude, gummy raspberries, and a never-ending supply of sock kibble[5] to genius-writer-friend Mega-Kate Boorman. She deserves combat pay for reading multiple drafts of this and everything else

---

2   This is a reference to the Greek myth of Sisyphus, a man who was cursed with having to push a boulder up a hill, only to have it roll back down again, for all eternity. Scholars believe it to be an ancient allegory about trying to get published.

3   That is not to say it is their fault when the the plot is—well—light, or I leave in ten thousand em dashes—I just like them.

4   I would talk more about them, but as I mentioned, it's Super Sekrit. Sorry.

5   Believe me when I tell you that you really don't want to know. Let's just say that in social situations, the best way to make a subtle escape is NOT to say you have to go and feed kibble to your sock. It will only end in confusion.

I write, not to mention putting up with Crazypants Mc-Flea when she makes an appearance. MK, you are my personal brand of Swedish Fish and I love you (platonically).

As for the inspiration, well, it knows no bounds. Or boundaries, really.[6] I have to first thank the elder Family Kirby, whose real-life shenanigans led to many Fletcher moments. Sadly, I often had to cut the best parts because readers felt "that could never really happen." Of course, with the Kirbys, it could and did. The Family Levy, while perhaps not as wild[7], are just as wonderful. Many thanks to my parents for making stories—from Winnie-the-Pooh to the Lord of the Rings—a cornerstone of my childhood. Also hugs and boop to most special sister Erica for sharing a lifetime of Cheerios books[8], among other things, and for loving everything I write, until I need her to edit it, when she turns into a red-pen-wielding shark[9]. I'm also ridiculously lucky to have an aunt who knows a little bit about writing kids' books[10]. Liz Levy has been a guide, cheerleader, and friend in need as I navigate the publishing world. She also buys me the best soup dumplings in New York, and for all of these things I am deeply grateful.

---

6   The inspiration keeps bugging me at dinner, or in the bathroom, you name it. I cannot escape.

7   We do not swing crowbars at miscreants on a playground, for example.

8   Cheerios book (noun): A beloved book that is read again and again, often while munching Cheerios right out of the box.

9   I know sharks don't have opposable thumbs. It's a metaphor.

10 She's written more than ninety of them. That's right. NINETY.

And finally there is my own sweet family. Pat, Noah[11], and Isabel[12], you have whistled and cheered and listened and stayed with me along this journey like the troop of ready travelers that you are. Thank you. Thank you. Thank you.

Last but not least, I must thank author extraordinaire Armistead Maupin. If, as a teenager, I had not discovered his *Tales of the City*, this tale might never have been written. This one's for Mouse.

---

11 Who, I should point out, does not barf all the time like his fictional namesake.
12 Nor does the real Isabel bite. Very often.

ABOUT THE AUTHOR

Dana Alison Levy was raised by pirates but escaped at a young age and went on to earn a degree in aeronautics and puppetry. Actually, that's not true—she just likes to make things up. This is why she has always wanted to write books. She was born and raised in New England, and studied English literature before going to graduate school for business. While there is value in all learning, if she had known she would end up writing for a living she might not have struggled through all those statistics and finance classes.

Dana was last sighted romping with her family in Massachusetts. If you need to report her for excessive romping, or if you want to know more, check out danaalisonlevy.com

Saying It
Out Loud

A Richard Jackson Book

Saying It
Out Loud

∾

a novel by Joan Abelove

A DK INK BOOK
DK PUBLISHING, INC.

A Richard Jackson Book

DK
Ink

DK Publishing, Inc., 95 Madison Avenue, New York, New York 10016

Visit us on the World Wide Web at http://www.dk.com

Library of Congress Cataloging-in-Publication Data
Abelove, Joan.
Saying it out loud / by Joan Abelove. — 1st ed.
p. cm.
Summary: With the help of her best friend, sixteen-year-old Mindy sorts through her
relationships with her solicitous mother and her detached father as she tries to come
to terms with the fact that her mother is dying from a brain tumor.
ISBN 0-7894-2609-9
[1. Mothers and daughters—Fiction. 2. Fathers and daughters—Fiction.
3. Death—Fiction. 4. Jews—United States—Fiction.]
I. Title.
PZ7.A1594Say 1999 [Fic]—dc21 98-33265 CIP AC

Book design by Annemarie Redmond.
The text of this book is set in 12 point Walbaum MT.

Printed and bound in U.S.A.

First Edition, 1999
4 6 8 10 9 7 5 3

Translation of "Locked In" from the Swedish "Innestängd" by Ingmar Gustafson, from *Half Sun Half Sleep*,
copyright © 1967 by May Swenson; used with permission of the Literary Estate of May Swenson. Quotations
on pages 4, 20, 62 from *The 13 Clocks*, copyright © 1950 by James Thurber. Quotation on page 11 from *The
Millions of Cats*, copyright © 1928 by Wanda Gág, 1956 by Robert Janssen. Quotation on page 12 from *The
Story of Ferdinand*, copyright © 1936 by Munro Leaf and Robert Lawson, 1964 by Munro Leaf and John W.
Boyd. Quotation on page 12 from *Horton Hatches the Egg*, copyright © 1940 by Dr. Seuss, 1968 by Dr. Seuss
Enterprises, L. P. Quotation on page 20 from *The Little Engine That Could* by Watty Piper, copyright © 1930,
1945, 1954, 1961 by Platt & Munk Co., Inc. Song lyrics on page 35 from "River, Stay 'Way From My Door" by
Mort Dixon and Harry Woods, copyright © 1931, 1958 by Callicoon Music. Song lyrics on page 40 from
"Accentuate the Positive" by Harold Arlen and Johnny Mercer, copyright © 1944, 1972 by Harwin Music Co.
Song lyrics on page 40 from "Mairzy Doats" by Milton Drake, Al Hoffman, and Jerry Livingston, copyright
© 1943 by Miller Music Corp. Quotation on page 42 from *J.B.*, copyright © 1956, 1957, 1958 by Archibald
MacLeish. Song lyrics on page 46 from "Runaround Sue" by Dion, copyright © 1961 by Bronx Soul
Music/Warner Chappell. Song lyrics on page 89 from "Take Good Care of My Baby" by Gerry Goffin and
Carole King, copyright © 1961 by Screen Gems/EMI Music. Song lyrics on page 116 from "Mama Said" by
Luther Dixon and Willie Denson, copyright © 1961 by Abkco Music, Inc. Song lyrics on page 116 from "Who
Put the Bomp" by Barry Mann and Gerry Goffin, copyright © 1961, 1989 by Screen Gems/EMI Music, Inc.

For Augusta

Locked In

All of my life I lived in a cocoanut.
It was cramped and dark.
Especially in the morning when I had to shave.
But what pained me most was that I had no way
to get in touch with the outside world.
If no one out there happened to find the cocoanut,
if no one cracked it, then I was doomed
to live all my life in the nut, and maybe even die there.
I died in the cocoanut.
A couple of years later they found the cocoanut,
cracked it, and found me shrunk and crumpled inside.
"What an accident!"
"If only we had found it earlier . . ."
"Then maybe we could have saved him."
"Maybe there are more of them locked in like that . . ."
"Whom we might be able to save,"
they said, and started knocking to pieces every cocoanut
within reach.
No use! Meaningless! A waste of time!
A person who chooses to live in a cocoanut!
Such a nut is one in a million!
But I have a brother-in-law who
lives in an
acorn

—*Ingemar Gustafson*
(translated by May Swenson)